Post Mortem Memoirs

POST MORTEM MEMOIRS

Short Stories

Errol Williams

Occam's Publishing ®
P.O. Box 230
Palm Harbor, Florida 34682

POST MORTEM MEMOIRS

Edited by Laverne Thompson and Kathleen Robison

Published by Occam's Publishing
P.O. Box 230
Palm Harbor, Florida 34682

Library of Congress Catoging-in-Publication Data

Williams, Errol
    Post Mortem Memoirs / Errol Williams.
ISBN 978-0-9788122-2-5

Second Edition: November 2017

Printed In the United States Of America

0 9 8 7 6 5 4 3 2

~ Acknowledgements ~

I would like to thank the following people for their help in completing this book:

Laverne Thompson, Kathleen Robison, Tracy Sieper, Denise Gauthier, Cheryl Endean, Jane and Andy Gorcica, Patti (Petunia) Caffio.

Thank you.

—Errol

DEVEN JAMES ULMER
Welcome to Planet Earth

In Memory Of
ELIZABETH ELAINE MCSHEA
1924 – 1974

We Miss you

For Cheryl Endean

The first person to encourage me to write

Migraine
19

Flicker of the Fireflies
31

Madman in the Moonlight
57

Flight of a Demon
79

Intangible Voices
95

Renina the Ice Dancer
111

Darkness of the Velvet Bed

Because of sickness, I close my eyes.
The crying of others fade to a soft, subtle wind.
I cannot move, peacefulness too overwhelming
I slip away—away from others at my side
on the manifested crying-wind of their sorrow.

The darkness is soft and accepting.
I used to fear her, I can't do that anymore.
How dare I ever fear something so natural,
the ticking of time wasted worrying
now it's over, I should have lived when offered.

In limbo, not here nor there, the darkness soft.
Intangible voices, echoes of betweenness
soft darkness, like laying in a warm wave, soft,
telling me it is time to go further
further than I already have gone.

I am awakened with consciousness
swooned with reality.
Now I see through the soft darkness.
The inside lid of a coffin
beautiful, but it cannot have me,
the darkness said so.

Pushing on the velvet lid, it does not move
touch of softness, hand slipping through
I feel the wet earth, cold, unforgiving
keeping my corpse, devouring—let me go!

I leave the darkness of the velvet bed,
soft earth touching my face
up, up through freshly disturbed dirt
until breaking through to moonlight waves.

The end of life is anew,
drifting the wave of moonlight forever.

ERROL WILLIAMS

Migraine

"Advil, where is my fucking Advil!"

It starts with a blind spot; an annoying speck of nothing obscuring the center of my peripheral view. It is hard to notice at first, it catches me off guard, sneaking up on me like the hideous, slithering python on its prey. Ever so silent and deceiving, however it's there, growing like a drop of oil in a dirty mud puddle on a pot holed, dirt road. Growing outward and annoying until I am overwhelmed with temporary blindness.

There is nothing you can do. Your day is shot, your plans, whatever they may have been—gone. Time to answer to the deformities of your head, nothing you can do now except hope that it's not too painful, hope to kill it with Advil before it gets you, hope it's over soon.

A migraine isn't something that happens to you, no, it is a creature, a billowing darkness, a loathsome entity that swims the consciousness of your mind, slithering the flow of your blood—clinging to the shadowy walls of your veins—hiding, waiting, for the right time to temporarily take over and make your life a living hell.

The stage of a migraine differs. Sometimes the blind spot fades, sometimes it doesn't. No matter what, the aura comes, a rippling in the darkness of your vision, you get a slight tinge of nausea, *be patient,* the tinge along with the aura grows, shutting your eyes can't shield you from it, you still see it, patterns of a sickening light weaving in the corner of your eye.

Did I mention the sweating? Sorry, I can't think straight; I am having a frigging migraine, thank you, it's not so much a sweat, but a wet, milky film that covers your body.

Mortality sucks.

The medicine cabinet for sure, that's where the fucking Advil is. No—wait, maybe under the fucking bed, I bet. Fingers growing numb, I can't stand that! Shit! Get control!

The pain is coming…

Are you ready?

Seven, eight, no—make it ten Advil, my liver will retaliate with a tight thumping sensation later, however it sure beats the feeling of my head squeezed in a vice.

Sleep, my dear friends, is your only salvation. If you can beat the dark storm to the land of nod, you win. Advil helps, however the migraine has a strong ally when it comes to this, its called anxiety. It works very well intensifying the nightmares in your room, keeping you awake with eyes wide, late at night. Yes I do speak from experience—sure not too be a dull evening.

One thing honorable about a migraine is the warning. It has the dignity of a British soldier in a red coat waving the Union Jack off in the distance, letting you know its coming to stick a bayonet into the side of your temple. Letting you think you do have some sort of chance to thwart the coming barrage—nope, sorry. You are still royally screwed. Trust me. I can guarantee it with a smile.

Outside the world is ugly. It's two a.m. and the rain is crashing hard against my house with the dreariness of the outside world intensifying the agony crawling up from the darkness of my body. The entity called Migraine is gathering, getting stronger as it courses through my veins, heading straight to the left side of my temple, slowly squeezing blood vessels until they seem to almost pop.

Here it comes, slow and steady, the pain is building.

Being partially blind—nauseated and sweating, I can see the bastard floating the corner of my room. The sporadic flash of lightning shows his outline drifting the darkness, silent and patient, riding the sickening aura in my eye.

He drifts closer, like a whirling cloud of smoke, or fog on a dismal night. In a blink, he is over me, for the side of my head feels like he is touching it with a hot finger, saying—here is where the fun will be....

His finger turns into a dagger. I feel his laugh vibrate through the tip piercing the first layer of skin of my temple. I feel blood drip like a tear down the side of my cheek, I do not move, the point digs deeper, the more you move the more it hurts. He surely knows this, all he has to do is hold the dagger steady, letting anxiety and restlessness do it's bidding. I try to push him away, I can see his shadow next to me, but my hand slides through thin air, the movement intensifies the pain—I hear him laugh—or is it the pain screaming in my head?

I—

I must have drifted off, most likely fainted; however, I am now feeling the full effects of my migraine. The side of my head feels as if I were smashed with a brick. I am sweating profusely, and where the pain pounds, it feels like warm blood dripping out of the side of my head. Lightning flashes extremely bright in my eyes, though half blind, the light still hurts horribly, enhancing the partial, peripheral blindness, making me brutally nauseous. The thunder echo runs through me like a frosted wind. The only salvation is the constant pounding of rain, the subtle, steady noise drowning out the dull silence of pain that is boiling the side of my head.

This migraine is the most horrific one I have ever had. Never have I seen the bastard materialized before my eyes, or is it mind? Am I imagining it? No! He is there in the darkness.

A dark figure, a solidifying, silhouette weaves into reality before me. His clothes smell like rot, dirt, his hand extended, his index finger pointing, touching—it is pure filth; I feel the unsanitary indentation it is doing to the side of my head. I can feel the diseased, bacteria's excitement of finding soft, warn flesh too crawl. I feel it shooting from his finger, an annoying itchy feeling as it makes way into my hair, ears, and eyes. I see them, like dark floaters swimming the retina of my eyes!

My head begins to ache with—

The pain is too much!

I slip into blackness.

* * *

The flash from the window surprised me; it woke me from a heavy, Advil induced sleep. How can there be lightening in December? I turn towards the window, squinting—the side of my head dull and thumping with migraine hangover.

The flash was not natural; it felt like an alien invader flashing a bright, white light outside my window. I waited patiently for the sudden jolt of thunder I thought would follow...

Nothing...

Instead, a low rumble rattled the windows, sending dust from the sills and an uneasy reality shooting through my body.

It seems an extremely warm, winter day, sunny, bright, how the sunshine dances—caressing and painting temporary abstracts on my wall. After that flash, that was as bright as a thousand sunny days, my world began to grow dark. My walls began crawling with shadows—in movement with the rolling, alien sound from a long distance away. A sense of anguish is flooding my meatless body. Something is terribly wrong. I do not have to look beyond my walls to know that.

I always found food to be an annoyance—too much of a bother, but now, suddenly I want a sandwich. I am not hungry mind you, but something arose in my stress level with a streaming sense of nervousness. As the shadows that are killing the sun follow me to the kitchen, faint screams and cries with blistering sounds of sirens are now bleeding through my walls—I do not believe the darkness brought them, I believe evil did. The very evil that is saturating my once bright walls.

I shake with sweat, chills shoot through me like a nail through a foot, it must be the after effects of the migraine—no, something else—something more. I am still in denial. My heart beats surprisingly slow but very hard, in my throat, not my chest. For some reason, I do not know why, I start to cry.

I turned on the television to a blurry screen and a steady hum. All the channels play the same tune. I take a bite from my ham sandwich and stare at the gray screen.

Outside pandemonium erupts over the steady static of the TV. I get up with burning agitation and fear, putting my ear to the wall, squishing my sandwich in my hand—listening.

Different and distinct horrors with a background ambiance of sirens come through my walls. My ear is so hard against it suction builds, almost popping my eardrum. Something is horribly, horribly wrong. I step back, looking at the wall as if it were a frightening phantom. I fall back in my chair, rubbing my brow with smashed white bread. It mixes with the pasty sweat that is pouring out of me. I jump from the chair and turn off the light, only the gray static from the TV is fluxing my room with gray matter everywhere, making it look like a million organisms crawling up my arms.

Then suddenly—

Beep, beep, beep, beep, came from the television. Long and strange sort of a beep and a whistle sound combined.

"This is the emergency broadcasting system: This is not a test, I repeat, this is not a test."

Snapping my head, my heart pounds, eye's wide to a now blue screen.

"Please stand by for an important, public announcement."

The screen is blue and solid, then turning back to a wintry snowstorm. I begin to shiver just looking at it, the tip of my nose is cold, fingers icy numb.

The sounds outside are growing steadily louder. I hear windows breaking, gunfire, car alarms, and—yes, a baby crying off in the distance.

More beeps and hums come from the TV. All my senses return to a solid blue screen. There is no face; there is no person to recognize on the screen. There is no one to look in the eye and share this hell that is happening.

"This is the emergency broadcasting system. This is not a test; I repeat this is NOT a test. News feed in thirty seconds. Please stand by"

The invisible speaker is solid, steady and unfeeling. He is hiding in the blue of my TV and he is detached from my reality. He is safe from a world unraveling.

Again:

"This is the emergency broadcasting system. This is not a test; I repeat this is not a test: Today, December 7, 2009, a nuclear device was detonated in the ship yards of lower Manhattan. The whole city and its surrounding boroughs have been turned into a fire ball and vaporized."

I get up to look out my kitchen window, it's snowing gray ash. It's snowing bits and pieces of New York City. I pull the shade down.

The horror from the blue screen continued:

"Four million people are believed to be dead from the horrific destruction that was unleashed on the United States; President John Hanson stated today this is a country-wide emergency and enacted Marshal Law over the entire country."

I turn off the TV. I can't take it anymore. I sit back in my chair, sinking deep into its silence. Rubbing my brow, pasting the beads of sweat smooth, I can feel my forehead glistening—it's hard to breathe. I start to focus on the sirens that are growing outside, suddenly all electricity goes dead in my house. The sound (Zziittt!) tells me it won't be on for a while, maybe never; time seemed to suddenly shut down. It's dark except for shredded, beams of light that break through the closed blinds covering my big picture window. Everything in my room is painted with dark shadows. The light bleeding from the shades pulls my attention. I turn my leather chair in its direction. I feel the cold leather stick to my body, gripping me tight, not letting the outside take me. Yes it's light, but different. It's tainted, dull and depressing—yet, I am drawn too it. I sit in my leather chair just looking at it, scared shitless, for that light touches the hell outside, and it's trying to enter my room and make me part of the chaos.

I just sit and watch the different shades of light grow lighter and darker, the longer I sit, the more dims and flickers explode from behind the curtain. It's alive, and I feel it breathing. I have not gone to open the shade and look out to see what has happened, what evil it covers with its existence.

Its speaking too me, I hear chattering rhetoric off in the distance, far away, slowly coming closer, growing louder to the point where I can make out the words. I cover my ears. I do not want to listen.

"Come see what you have done."

"I can't."

"Come see what your sniffling, spineless rat bastard of a civilization has done too this beautiful world."

"I didn't—"

"Shut up!"

"Come look, that's all I am asking. Take a peek. Take a look. Look now or I'll—"

Bang! Bang! Bang!

My head turned so hard I hurt my neck. Someone angrily is banging on my front door, my heart begins pounding in my chest. I sit in the darkened room, a moment of silence, a moment of stillness, the only disruption coming from the world behind the shade.

Again: BANG! BANG! BANG!

My heart jumps again.

"Ah, I can see this is going too be a fun game, your kind invented it, nurtured it, now you don't want too play."

"If you won't look out and see what the human race had done, then I guess it wants to pay you a visit."

"No."

"You might as well look, your life is over. This isn't September 2001, however horrific that was, it is minute from this, your team went far beyond the call of duty, I am afraid this is permanent my friend. There will be no bouncing back. This is it, game over, your team wins, but you get no trophy and can't go home ever!"

"I—"

"Choose!"

My head is spinning. The inside shell of my chest is ice; I feel my heart trying to keep running, pumping harder and harder, trying not to stop in the artic freeze surrounding it—I am shivering. I turn my head to the door, and then look back at the fraying lights from behind the blinds.

BANG! BANG! BANG! BANG!!!

Getting up is daunting. I feel the cold leather of the chair peel from my skin like Velcro, making a sucking sound as I get up. The hallway is dark with just enough natural light too make out the doorway leading to the staircase. I hear a heavy rattling at the door, I can hear the doorknob twist and violently jerk, then more banging. I move slowly, swallowing hard to keep my heart out of my throat, nonetheless I keep going down the hall. I turn the corner atop the stairs, shivering with fear, hiding in the darkness of the landing. In the hall below, I see a huge shadow filling the shade covering the solid windowpane of the front door. If this thing wants in, it can easily do so, yet, it just moves violently banging the door and gripping the doorknob with sheer ferocity.

"What are you waiting for?" Something said from thin air.

"It's a manifestation of you. So you think, so you create. Isn't this what you humans wanted? At that door is your kind in all its glory, your spirit, and your achievements. Why not go and enjoy the manifestations of a destructive mind?"

"Shut up!"

"Nagasaki and Hiroshima were not enough; you just had to keep going."

"Shut up!"

"God created the Earth, and then Man. Man created It, and killed the Earth—bravo!"

"Shut your fucking mouth!"

"And now your little pet is killing you. All of you!"

"Aaaaarrrrhhhhhh!"

I scream holding my temples. Its voice echoes the walls of my head. This has to be a nightmare, this cannot be happening!

"You're right, it's not happening, no, no, no. It's done! Sign, sealed delivered."

CRASH!

The window down stairs finally shattered. A loud whirling sound came from below. I slam the upstairs door and bolt it, stepping back. Instantly something not human began pounding it. Strange growls and cries came from the other side. I am unraveling. I feel the dagger once more in my skull. I ran back to the picture window, I tear away the shade and in that instant, all the windows of my home explode. A kaleidoscope of shimmering glass fills the air. I feel the glass break skin all over my body; it feels like a thousand stingers from angry hornets. I feel the warm blood flow, getting in my eyes and mouth; I feel heat of a nuked world engulfing me.

Outside the world is burning. I see people running on fire; I see the eyes of man wide with sheer terror. Outside my window, it's playing different scenes and images of other places around the world. Russia, China, Australia, Europe, all engulfed in a wicked flame of hell. I am staring at the Empire State Building from angle unknown. I watch the massive structure crumble into a sea of fire, all being viewed with the sounds of sirens and screams playing as the background music. It's amazing how it plays together perfectly. The Devil's play is unfolding, I am standing in ash and ruins of a worlds' stage crumbling, the final act of humankind.

As the world dies before my eyes, after viewing the hell unleashed outside my body, I feel my insides begin to unweave. The external ramification is now finishing the job internally that we humans let happen.

I notice hair falling on my shoulders. Grabbing handfuls from my head, it came out as easily as pulling a tissue from a tissue box. I look at it for a second, letting it drop like dead petals from a dandelion, it sizzles and disappears before hitting the floor. I watch my fingernails curl up and burn. Horrible brown spots began covering my skin. I feel my eye lids melt away from the searing heat. I cannot blink anymore; the daunting sensation of trying to shut them is frustrating. Nonetheless the feeling passes. For now the nuclear fallout has eaten my eyes. All I see is white….

*   *   *

It has gone. The hell that engulfed me is gone. I am in my room floating, looking down on my living room. There are men in suits moving and looking, surrounding a black, canvas body bag on the floor. I know that bag all too well: it's a Postmortem, Crime Scene Recovery bag. Guaranteed to keep blood borne pathogens and bodily fluids contained, it comes with a blessing from OSHA. We keep them stocked at the lab for "emergencies".
I know it's me. I know it's my body outlining the interior of that bag.

I listen:

"Name: Dr. James Killjoy."

"Date of birth: 12-3-56"

"Occupation: Physicist"
"Cause of Death: Aneurism"

I just watch quietly as they go about their business, chatting about the game, kids, wives, mother-in-laws and other dissatisfactions in their lives. Once again, the world is alive and beautiful and I am mystified. I have a sudden urge to leave; a beautiful bluish-white light up in the distance of my room is calling me. A beautiful white light is off in a cloud-obscured distance. The feeling is overwhelming, calling me to come—I can't. I look down on the black bag that lies on my carpet; its sullen and still, inside the cool darkness is the corpse of me. It feels like I am leaving an old friend, or relative. Again, the light gives me a silent call to come, yet I still cannot go, I turn to look at it, I feel it's warmth, but can only shake my head and look at the canvas body bag there like a throw rug. I float down, through one of the detectives in my way; it felt like slipping into a warm bath. I see him shiver from touching the outline of my new existence, shaking off the chill he returns to his business. I pass through him and touch the black, canvas bag. I lay down on top feeling the outline of my dead corpse, and then slipping into the fathoms of its reality—like lying down in a murky puddle. I feel my old cold, dead body engulf my entity like a cocoon. I feel a cold heart that will not pump warm blood; I feel wet lungs filled with some watery puss that will not let air pass through ever again.

Even though I cannot come back to life, fine, I am more than ok with that, nonetheless this cold, dead body is reassuring; it always was, even though I let it down, I miss it deeply—it's a hard habit to break. It's dark in here and very cool. I feel the inside lining of latex touching my already decomposing face, and draping my lifeless body. The bag is cold and somewhat damp. I know I should go to the light, but for now, I am going to stay here with an old friend and reminisce....

FLICKER OF THE FIREFLIES

"Attention passengers, LKM, flight 642 will be boarding shortly." A static ridden voice moaned from a distant, dark corner of the airport.

John Roth sighs getting up from a hard, blue chair, almost tripping over the yellow mop bucket catching the wet misery from a stained ceiling tile in the airport waiting room. Heading towards the window he looks out onto the dark, runway trying to escape the stench of an old cigar lingering the already stale air. No, you're not allowed to smoke in the airport but being late at night, some bastard was getting away with murder.

Staring out onto the tarmac, he notices the dark, silhouette of his outline in the window. Seeing his reflection in the glass, he stares at the old, gaunt man looking back at him. Touching the wrinkles near his eyes that web outward to leather tough, sun

torched skin—he sighs. The whites of his eyes that were once
clear and beautiful now have a yellowish discharge that glisten in
the glass with a road map of red, bloodshot lines floating in them.
His receding hairline rides back to grayish, black hair making his
forehead look very large with strange, protruding, growths dotting
it from years in the hot sun. "I'm old." He mutters, trying to clear
the stench of the lingering cigar. Thank God, this will be all over
soon.

The weather outside this airport window is horrible. He cringes
looking through the waggles of water dripping down the window
at the soaking, wet plane that he is about to board. It's out there
eerily in the night, deep in the darkness, hauntingly dim, and five
hours behind schedule. Some say because of obviously bad weather, others mention a technical issue not fully explained. As usual,
there is no straight answer from the airlines.

Bastards…

John rubs his stomach staring at the shadows darting and twisting around the fuselage, flashlights ride the wings and tale sections
looking for something. They say its nothing when asked about the
long delay and the wild flashes of light dancing on the plane outside in the night. With a look of irritation and stale smile, they say:
"We will be leaving shortly, please be patient!"

You got to love LKM.

Bastards….

This trip to the Netherlands will be his last. Retiring early has
been his dream and after this less-than-a-week endeavor it will become a reality. It's been such a long ride and now his little house
in Rhode Island is on the horizon of his minds eye. However,
knowing he has got to get on that plane just one more time is shear
torture. A nauseating feeling in the back of his throat and this feeling is nothing new. It has crawled there many times just before

boarding his flights, and why should tonight be any different. Flying has always tormented John, and tonight it's even worse than ever before. Maybe because of the storm, maybe because this is his last trip, his flights to Europe have always been at night, which, just add to his misery. He just can't put his finger on it. The plane is packed and darker than usual. The lights are dim and flickering on one side of the jet from front to back. John stops, looking at the light show overhead, dancing lights have him captivated. He turns to ask the stewardess without saying a word, she responds: "There is a slight electrical problem" With a sarcastic smile, she went back to greeting the walk-ons.

The air is thick as paste, its stuffy, and feels like being at the bedside of a dying friend. He is distraught; this is not a good attitude to have just after boarding late at night, with a six-hour flight a head of you, through the darkness over the Atlantic Ocean. He can't help himself, though all his past travels were flawless, he can't get rid of the haunting feeling when he flies. "It's been too perfect" he muttered low and to himself. However, he tries to shake the bad thoughts running wild in his mind. He read a long time ago, if you have just one bad experience, you will never, ever have a bad experience again. The chances are that slim and that's if anything happens at all.

Those have got to be the words of non-flyers, dick-wad pencil pushers.

The sad thing is that nothing ever happened—yet.

Bastards....

They say, every day there are sixty thousand planes in the air at any given time, and that is just in America! "Hogwash!" John said aloud, the person next to him shooting him a strange look. John must play these tidbits of airplane statistics over and over in his head or he would never fly.

But soon it will all be over. He will be in Holland for less than a week, then a little local fieldwork when he gets back to the states and that's it. Thirty-eight years of traveling and that is it! "I will never fly again!" He said to himself, but looking out of the wet, window from his seat, no doubt this will be a long, long flight.

The 747-300 is frightening. It seems smaller than usual and very old. It reminds him of an old school bus he used to ride when he was a kid. Smoking was banned almost twenty years ago, yet there is a worn out, heavily used ashtray under his arm, continuously reminding him how old this piece of shit with wings really is. Suddenly John is overwhelmed to sniff the seat in front of him, still, to this day stale smoke reeks from the fabric. Sweat began to bead on John's forehead, with a palpitation in his chest.

The people on board seem pale and preoccupied in their thoughts, lost or frightened by something swimming through their mind, the feeling sent chills through Johns' body. He can sense the anxiety of everyone in the plane—a strange camaraderie lingers the stale air of the cabin. The scratchy, highly flammable fabric of the chair scrunched John's shirt, not to mention the arms of the chairs that were not designed for anyone over 5' 3". And here we go, ready to fly into the night in an old, relic bus with wings.

A large thump echoed the fuselage. John's heart sank to his stomach as the gate pulled away. He laughed; he is already scared shitless and they were not even off the ground yet. Finally the plane started to taxi the runway. The plane seemed to wobble, moving out on the tarmac, as if they were riding on one oval tire. He could only shake his head. All he could do now is sit back and watch the flickering light show over his head. The sweat ran down his nose. "Son of a bitch!" He said, over and over.

The worst thing about flying is the waiting on the tarmac. You can be there for a minute, or an eternity depending on how long they want to torment you. In addition to the storm, you could bet it will be awhile. However to John's surprise, the plane began to

roll. The runway at JFK started to rumble John's seat. He felt
the vibrations through his whole body—he grips the chair so hard
there are pieces of dried out fabric under his fingernails. A strange
feeling ran through his feet, "Was that a damn pothole?" John
cried, of course no one heard. But then the bumpy roll smoothed.
They started to ark upwards and with a sharp dip to the right they
were off, heading into a curtain of darkness.

Leveling off at thirty-six thousand feet used to ease John a
bit, they say that ninety percent of all mishaps happen on takeoff
and landing, however, the flickering lights were really starting to
get too him. The people also seemed uneasy and sweating. It is
unusually hot and there is no air flowing from the vents over head,
and with the lights flickering, he is suddenly engulfed with anxiety.
Getting the attention of the flight attendant wasn't easy. She probably didn't see him or more likely she was ignoring him outright.
Finally with a roll of her eyes she glanced over and seemed an-
noyed by his agitation. John pointed to the lights, put his hands in
the air with a shrug, she rolled her eyes, shook her head in a way
he did not comprehend, making no sense at all, she turned away.
John sat back, tingling with frustration; he fumbled some more
with the switch, and then giving up all together.

The plane is definitely darker than any plane he was on before,
darker, with a dreariness John never experienced in his many years
of flying. Something did not feel right; something surreal is eating
at his nerves. The turbulence is inevitable, but worse there is a
thumping sound echoing inside the cabin. The thumping was not
too loud, but any strange sound always calls your attention when
you are thirty-six thousand feet in the air. A flicker of green came
from a black, oval window a couple of seats up and across the
aisle—John's eyes glistened with curiosity. The guy sitting there
is sound asleep, not seeing the flash from the window. John was

hesitant, but the curiosity was too overwhelming—to strong. He needed to get the horrible turbulence off his mind. As the rest of the people were lost in chatter from the strange thumps happening in different locations of the plane, they did not notice John moving across the aisle. He sat next to the sleeping man and looked out the black oval of the window. He froze with eyes bulging. A face in the window, a green, mutilated face, wet from the drenching rains, glaring at him from outside.

Johns' blood drained from his body. He almost collapsed in the seat, waking the sleeping man. "Are you all right?" The man asked. John just nodded and sat back. It was only there for an instant, but he'd seen it. Concern came over him; he tried to process what just had happened. I'm "tired" John thought, looking back at the blackness of the window. Seeing ghosts at thirty six thousand feet is incomprehensible, but who the ghost was even more unbelievable.

Tom Flicker.

Looking up, something sounds like thunder rolling over the fuselage above. No, not thunder, heavy footsteps running the length of the plane, getting the attention of other passengers as well. Seeing the looks on their faces, he sinks deep into his chair. He knows it's real, they know it's real from the look in their eyes; they're hearing it too. John tries to calm down, "It was only thunder," he said. Tom Flicker is dead, and it was only thunder!

* * *

"You can run, Flicker, but you can't hide!"

A boy peddling with mad ferocity felt words of hate thump his back. He never peddled so hard, or cried so much in his life. "Leave me alone!" cried the boy, wiping the tears and snot from his freckled face, trying to keep his balance, trying to get away. Hearing the laughter of the bullies getting closer, he peddled harder barely staying ahead, because the wind and his bicycle are his enemy. The bent rim of his Schwinn is rubbing against the forks, with a few more unexpected potholes, it's even worse than before. Tears are flowing from his eyes, and it is so hard to breathe, probably do to the fact that unconsciously he is grinding his teeth with uncontrolled anger. The anger in him goes far beyond the thugs chasing him. It's been a long and unforgettable weekend. Even in his fear right now, he still can see his mother in that coffin, stiff, cold, and pale. She died last Thursday from a long and horrible illness that is still running in his mind continuously. He remembers the last time she came from the hospital, he was so happy, his mother was better and now everything would be fine. Still, there was a feeling, something not right. The last day she came home, she was distant, absorbed by something that living and healthy people cannot see. The lipstick she used to apply with such precision that made her the most beautiful mother in the world was slapped on carelessly and uneven, as if put there by the hand of a child. She seemed to be slightly hunched over, and spoke with aspirated breaths. Her touch was distant, cold and foreboding in every way you could imagine. The hospital bed in the living room should have been a dead giveaway, however, not to a young boy. At night, he could hear her cry, it would echo through the house. Later on, when his father went to bed, he would sneak down the stairs, watching her from the darkness of the hallway. All lights would be out but for one white candle. She was in so much pain, so much agony—even her shadow from the candle's light seemed to be climbing the wall to the ceiling trying and escape but it can't, it cannot tear away from the sick woman's soul.

She loved white, everything white. He held back tears remembering how she used to dress him in white all the time. Even the happiness seemed white then, now it is all gone, except for the light of one white candle illuminating the darkness of a sick and tired woman—a mother who was loosing the battle of her worst nightmares. Tom went back upstairs, passing his fathers room where he can hear him snoring without a care in his bones. He hated his father, he hated everything about him. His uncaring ways made Tom hate him with a passion. Back in his room, Tom stared at the ceiling listening to the cries and sorrows of a mothers end. They reeked through the vents and every crack and crevasse of his room. Long into the night he listened, he wanted to go to her, but he couldn't, he could not face the fact he was loosing her. So he stayed, stayed in his little room just above where his mother lay dying. After a while, the cries became softer and Toms eyes though wet with tears grew heavy and finally, the boy was able to sleep. He woke up late the next day, lost in a heavy fog. No one woke him for school, something is wrong. He dressed then hurried down the stairs to the living room where he found the empty hospital bed, his mother was gone. He ran to the kitchen and out the back door and there stood his father, watching a Hearse pull out of the driveway. Tom collapsed to the ground.

His Father, shed no tears, her wake on Friday, buried on Saturday, and Tom Flicker was back to school on Monday.

And life goes on.

He turns down Cook's Lane. Not the brightest thing to do but believe it or not, his mind was elsewhere. It's a four-mile dirt road, lined on both sides with apple trees as far as the eyes can see. Vreeman's Apple Orchard is a six-generation family farm in Towaco. They started with a couple of acres and then grew, swallowing up the land around them, eventually growing to over three hundred acres.

The hot, August day is turning to dusk. The boy-thugs chasing Tom are having a hard time seeing through the haze of the hot day, but Tugboat, the nastiest hooligan of them all, refuses to lose Tom from his sight, he will not let him go. Anger is in his eyes, sweating too much candy and soda pop from his young, obese body. He leans forward on his bike, trying to make his fat body as aerodynamic as possible. However, this is hard to do with your belly hanging out over the handlebars and your shirt riding up, flapping in the wind like a warning flag on the back of a wide-load truck. The grin on his face says it all, he is out for Tom, and nothing is going to stop him!

The gang turns down Cooks Lane with Tom in their imaginary crosshairs of the handlebars. Sweat is pouring from their bodies. The hot, sticky afternoon is unforgiving, making the dust of the road stick to their faces. The grit in their teeth doesn't slow them down, only adds to the thrill of the hunt.

"He fell!" Said a lost voice in the pack. In the distance, the sun is setting fast, but not yet dark enough to see Tom abandon his bike on the side of a gully where he fell. There was laughter from the pack and Tugboat bellowed the loudest. "You can run, but I will get you, Flicker!" "Take it like a man!" The other boys just looked at each other and smirked, wondering if fat boy was in the sun to long. John, the youngest in the bunch, looked at his brother, but Keith just shrugged, and brought his bike to a stop.

The darkness seems to be creeping in fast, with the sun just under the mountain, the path Tom ran down is even darker. The smell of rotten apples fills the air as the hunt for Tom Flicker commences on foot. The path is shrouded with eerie brush and the kids hesitate, but enter anyway. "If that pussy can go in so can we!" The fat one sang.

The path leads to Weavers pond where the sunfish are wild, and the lilacs kill the smell of rotten, old apples that fill the August night. And, most of all, the home of Gretchen, the oldest apple tree in New Jersey. It was planted by great grandpa Vreeman more then a hundred years ago. The family is baffled as to how she can still be alive for so many years, even with her fruit-bearing years behind her, she still sprouts leaves every spring. She is not your normal apple tree by any means. She is much bigger than the average apple tree. They say old man Vreeman bought the seeds from a gypsy and they were cursed, of course no one believed it. Vreeman had a strange sense of humor and laughed like hell when ever someone would mention it. However, nonetheless, Gretchen is the strangest apple tree in all of New Jersey.

An owl hoots and the boys turn to see eyes glowing in the trees. They swallow hard, but the darkness of the path is calling them, and sure as there is a devil, they do not want to go. The stench of rotten apples is eminent; it's under their feet, smashing into the treads of their Keds. Then they heard it, through the darkness, over the noise of the crickets coming out for the evening, and the sunfish breaking water, they heard the whimpering of a child. Under the haunting shadows of Gretchen lays a boy against her in the fetal position, like a grandmother trying to sooth a child, Tom Flicker, sobs softly.

The gang moves slowly towards him. Not focusing on Tom, but the haunting aura of how Gretchen stands over the crying boy. The knots in her trunk look like ears listening to their ever cautious moves and conversations, her shadows stretch deep to the sky, her branches are raised claws ready to slash down at them any moment. Granted that was strange to the gang, but not as strange as the lightning bugs dancing around Flicker and the tree that he is under. They stood looking at each other, mesmerized at the phenomena floating around Tom's body. With the hot evening breeze drying the sweat on there foreheads, they move closer.

"Who's gonna save ya now" curdled off Tugboats tongue.

"Who's gonna save little Tom Prickster now?"

As Tugboat got close, Tom began to fidget and whimper louder. When Tug tried to grab him, Tom kicked and slashed in a spastic frenzy, then curled back up into a ball. Tugboat tried to grab him, but the sweat and the speed of Tom's unruly manners made this nearly impossible.

The Tug stood confused. He's never gone this far, outside of just verbally abusing Tom or any other vulnerable kids from school. He turned to see the others waiting in anticipation of what he will do, but all fat boy could do was perspire, nervously. He didn't know what to do. He felt the rotten apples under his feet, and then it hit him while twisting the apples with his foot into the soft earth. He turned to the gang with a grin and said: "Grab his arms!"

The boys looked at each other—then did what they were told. They hesitated moving under Gretchen, but found the nerve from Tugboats glare. The boys each pulled a limb from his balled-up body. Tom went wild. Crying and trying to kick, just going absolutely mad. The kids were startled by his lunatic manners, but they held firm, because they were even more afraid of the fat one.

As the boys subdued Tom as best they could, fat boy held the most rotten apples in all of Towaco. They were pure mush in his blubbery fingers. Standing over the boy, he smeared the dead, rotten apples in Tom's hair. Wet, soggy apple puss drips down Flickers crew cut. The exhausted boy just lay there, breathing heavy. Not seeming to bother and maybe a little at ease that this might be the brunt of his humiliation. As he lay there wheezing from asthma, hoping they would be satisfied and maybe a little sympathetic, they would leave. But the bullies were going nowhere.

Tugboat is lost in immature thoughts of what to do next. A

light, flickering green glow has grabbed his attention. "Get me his news bag!" he said, looking at little John Roth, the youngest of the bunch, and the only one watching the trashing of Tom Flicker, being to young to be of any help, Tug finally found use for him.

He looked at his brother for guidance but Keith was too busy wrestling a leg, so he did what he was told.

There, next to the blue Schwinn, was a bag for paperboys that read, (The Daily Tribune) in bright, blue lettering with red outline. The fabric of the bag was glowing; it would flash green, brighter then darker, almost pulsing a green, alien glow. No evening paper ever did that! As little John walked toward the boys, they could not help but stare at the bag. What could it possibly be? There minds swam with curiosity, there imaginations were soaring. Tom began to flinch, then to jerk harder, making the gang focus more at their job at hand. "Don't touch that!" The boy cried. Slowly he brought the bag to Tugboat, as he did little Johns' body began to glow shades and ambiances of green. The boys looked on, a little frightened, the bag clanked as he walked towards Tug boat, handing it too him, he was hesitant, but he took it. The boys gasped, wondering what the fat-one will find. Tug was nervous when he opened the flap, then a smirk ran across his face with a green tint from the content of the bag, making him look like a green goblin on Halloween.

"Well, well. What do we have here?" "It looks like we were interrupting dinner." "Are you hungry, Tom?" Tugboat pulled out two mason jars filled with lightning bugs, thousands upon thousands of little creatures crawling up and down the interior of the glass. It flickered and glowed like a lantern with weak batteries. "Are you hungry Tom?" Fat boy said un-screwing the lid, barely getting his fat hand in the mouth of the jar, and only because he was sweating. Getting it out was another story. He couldn't. Tom seen this and through sobbing eyes, started to giggle, with the gang beginning to smirk themselves. This infuriated fat boy while struggling to free his hand; his face was ballooning red with anger.

The jar was glowing bright when out of anger fat boy's fist clenched. The jar shattered, sending lightning bugs free into the air, the lucky ones anyway. Blood dripped down his arm, with the glass at his feet. Tugboat now had a bracelet of glass. The other boys never saw him raw with anger before. His eyes were bulging as he walked over to Tom. The dead bugs in his hand were a green, glowing glob. He smeared it all over Flickers face, on his neck, in his ears and even his eyes. As Tom was crying, fat boy also managed to get it in his mouth. Toms face is now glowing florescent green, bright as a bug zapper. He lay there stoic and in shock, twitching sporadically. It was a disturbing sight to see.

Tom suddenly went absolutely mad, exploding into a violent fit. All the boys together could not hold him down any longer—letting him go, releasing him as Tom lost all his humanity. He charged fat boy, who put his hands up in a cowardly fashion and Tom slipped on rotten apples before he even had gotten to Fat Boy. As he fell, his hands caught him, but they found the shattered, glass jar. The newly formed cuts overflowing with blood were deep canyons of torn flesh. He was lost now in pure madness. His eyes were rivers of tears. The boys were taken back, stunned; this has gotten way out of hand. Even fat boy was lost in the frenzy.

Tom went running off screaming like a madman. His head was glowing, with green trails following him. He ran straight through the apple trees, branches scaring his face, tearing his shirt, into the dirt road where he met the grill of the grandson of old-man Vreeman's sixty-five Dodge. There was no screeching of tires because tires can't screech on dirt. Tom's young body twisted and rolled under the truck. The boys ran to the spot where the headlights stopped bouncing in the dust filled, dirt road. Tom's blurry face began to show through the settling dust. The glow of his face was coming from underneath the truck. A strange odor is riding the wind of this August night. It was the smell of burning flesh from his limp mangled body underneath the chassis. The transmission and muffler were hot, causing the flesh to sizzle like bacon. His glowing, green face made the blood oozing out of his nose and ears look like black tar. Calmness was in his open eyes that were staring straight ahead into darkness.

Tom Flicker was dead....

The blackness outside the window was haunting. John stared at the outlined, dark reflection looking back at him. His own brother's death came flooding in his mind. By the time Keith died, the rest of the gang was long gone. Oh, how they died so hideously. Tugboat was hit by the 6:40 coming out of New York City just pulling into The Towaco Rail Station. The girl behind the counter of Bob's Deli said he came in, looking frightened, asked for a train schedule, and turned without even saying thank you.

The train was just pulling in when it hit him, pulling him under slowly, swallowing him like a Hoover vacuum. The screams echoed long into the evening, body parts everywhere, the witnesses were surprised there was enough of him left to make such horrible sounds. It was horrifying knowing that he was under that train in pieces screaming bloody murder. However, eventually the screaming died, and so did Tugboat. Finally, when the night was quiet once more, they were able to move the train to gather the remains. When they did get what was left of him, there was only an arm, torso, and head intact, and to everyone's surprise, he was still alive—barely. You couldn't make out what he was saying because one side of his jaw was ripped clean off, bone and neck muscles keeping the horror on his face.

* * *

Keith was the last to go. John and the rest of his group thought he was having a bad trip. Being rebellious teenagers and dropping four-way blotter will do that to you.

Camping at the watershed was a normal occurrence in the hot summers in Lake Hiawatha, New Jersey. Genesee Cream Ale was the beer of choice back then; cheap, God was it cheap, a high school students dream. You could by a joint and a six-pack all with just your lunch money. Those were the good old days.

The stars out that night shimmered like bright diamonds on a black, velvet cloth. Yes, the acid was kicking in, along with Keith's intolerable paranoia. They heard a lot of things strolling the woods that night, but nothing as to what Keith was hearing. They knew the trip was coming on, but it seemed a little premature. Maybe there was a little tingling in your fingers. Maybe a little flair of light in the corner of your eye, but it was definitely too early for the full bang. He was the eldest of the two boys, the hero, and the one who never lost control, yet tonight he is transfixed on the woods, his mind is unraveling. Like he was watching demons' dance in the tree line—maybe he was!

They partied hard into the night. Swirling, purple lights swam on the water of the reservoir. Bright, silvery fish sporadically jumped through the air for low flying bugs, breaking the dark mirror of water. They laughed, and sang to the eight-track blaring with low batteries. Everyone was having a great time, except for Keith. His wide eyes were on the woods—something out there was scaring the shit out of him. The sweat of paranoia pouring from him said so. It is a bad omen to be around someone having a bad one, so they decided to go down to the dam. Letting Keith deal with his demons seemed the thing to do. When tripping, paranoia is contagious like the flu. If one has it, it is easily spread, so the unanimous vote is to head to the dam. One thing that seems to help in preventing the "trip induced: paranoia is noise. Yes it's true, and the waterfall at the edge of the dam produces plenty of non-paranoia, beautiful noise!

The dam is long and narrow, power lines stretch the length of it on one side and you must watch it because they're only six-feet off the edge, one might think that is a lot of room for a young healthy kid with dexterity, but not when you are tripping. They feed power to the massive pumps that open and close the gate of the waterfall. Among the group this was understood, so down the dirt road they went, leaving Keith staring, now into the blazing campfire with sudden jerks over his shoulder looking into the tree line.

"I can't believe he is just going to sit there by himself." Tina, one of the locals said. "The candy we ate, you definitely don't want to be alone staring into a roaring fire." But the fire was not on his mind; it was a howling from the woods only Keith could hear.

The road was dark, but traveling with fellow trippers was an electrifying experience. Even though it was August, there was a soft, cool breeze drifting the waters with the full, white moon, lighting their way. The moon's light was casting fantastic, geo-metric shapes, through the treetops along the path that twisted and turned as they moved down it. Different patterns of moonlight would shift and move like a forgotten disco globe of the seventies.

The lightning bugs were blinking in the dark, thick foliage. The soft wind felt like velvet touching their faces with the smell of lilac blending in its invisible currents. Yes it was a beautiful night; the bullfrogs and crickets were singing their chorus, and the world was right for once for these young, teenage partiers. Now it was time for a purple ride, a journey enjoyed by the young, rebellious, parent hating, acne faced kids with all the answers, a sharing in something their parents refuse to understand, everyone here was beginning to see the lights of unnatural realities, brought on from the derivatives of rat poison.

Where the dirt road ends at a big rock half lying in the water, they made a sharp right, down a path that ran the waterline. The sandy path felt strange to their feet, it is alive, grabbing their toes. The sound of the waterfall filled their ears. It was a very wet summer, so the dam was open often, and tonight was no exception. The path ended at an open field, with the dam one hundred feet in front of them. The sky looming over the water was beautiful. The moon was full and changing colors from blue, to green, to a dark red. The open waters were breaking deep purples and bright silver. Everything was slowing now. Time is tripping by, with the stars dripping overhead.

The next thing they knew it was passing midnight. You couldn't see the faces of your fellow partyers but they were there. Ghost-like silhouettes against the darkness, except when they dragged on their smoke, their faces would glow soft reds, yellows and oranges, like toothless jack-o'-lanterns on Halloween. The trail of lit cigarettes left from dark shadows illuminating in the moonlight was intriguing, absorbing, mesmerizing, sending chills up the spine. Led Zeppelin was playing on the eight-track to the roar of the waterfall into the surprisingly cool August night. Joints were lit, and eyes were as bright as the glow of the roach being past back and forth from pumpkin head to pumpkin head, holding long hits, letting it out slow with long exhales, the grey trails of smoke in the moonlight floating up, twisting and twirling to the stars.

However, the good times came to an end with a bright green flash from the woods. The green light seemed to hover, slowly moving over the top of the trees. Suddenly from nowhere, over the roar of the waterfall, a horrible scream and a splash! The blotter trip was heavy and everything was oh, so slow. John's brother was in the water swimming towards them, gasping for air. He came to shore screaming like a lunatic, "Get him away from me!" Keith passed the crowd and headed for the dam. John stood in shock. A bright green flare coming from the woods looking like a fire, but it couldn't be a fire, being that it was bright green. As the crowed watched the green flare some oohed and aahed at the spectacle happening, another bright like flared in the opposite direction. This time it was a fire. Keith tangled himself in the power lines of the dam. He was trying to scream, but the electricity running through him was only letting out gurgling sounds of pain. His eyes were wide staring into an empty void, as though looking at the devil himself. His hair was straight with trails of smoke before he finally let go—falling to the concrete. The group screamed and scattered in all directions, John ran to his smoldering brother's side, but there was nothing he could do. The distortion of his face was too much for John and he had to turn away, and that is when he had seen him. He thought it was the trip at the time but now he knows. At the edge of the water he saw him—Tom Flicker, in the bushes at the waters' edge, smiling and green-faced, just looking at John. He can feel the evil touching deep within his soul, sending a fear through him like he never experienced before. He didn't know what to do—he is lost in the confusion. The sound of sirens began to echo off the dam. Reality slowly began seeping back into John. The face near the water began to distort and melt into the water. A green glow, like an oil slick, began to move up the tree line of the reservoir, like a slithering snake. The green flashes in the woods now are a bright orange—the woods were ablaze.

John sat in the police car watching the covered body of his

brother. He just stared into the night, the trip has faded and reality is slamming John hard. As he stared at the fading rainbow of the night, the word fell from his lips. "Flicker."

* * *

Keith died a long time ago, and the rest followed soon after. Joe, Timmy, Franklin, and fat-ass died under strange circumstances and now, what ever this thing is, it's after John.

John could only stair into space. Anxiety ran through him like a spike driven through his chest with a sledge hammer. His eyes rolled upwards in a single movement. The lights overhead dimmed following a loud thumping noise coming from the side of the airliner over the roar of the troubled turbines. Everyone's head turned with shrieks of despair, their heads bouncing back and forth, trying keep what ever is in their stomachs down from the heavy turbulence. Everyone was lost in a haze of horror. Strange, horrible sounds rang through the fuselage in time with the bouncing of the plane, as though someone is dancing to the shaking rhythm. Eye's followed the creaking and twisting sounds that echoed everywhere along the interior of the plane. But John knew different. Green flickers of light illuminated the black, oval windows across from him. No one else seems to notice, but he knew what it was. A nightmare from long ago, something to hideous to understand was dancing the clouds, and he was calling John to come and be his partner. Across from him, the row of seats are empty. As the lights dimmed in and out of darkness, he moves to the empty seats riding the wing.

He stares out the window. He knows he is out there in the darkness, the sweat puddles and streams down his face. The anxiety is overwhelming but John looks and swallows hard. Out in the pouring rain, on a soaking wet wing stands Flicker. The silhouette of a monster against the storming clouds behind him, like a black and white photo except for his face. It glows green—an incandescent glow riding the clouds. His eyes are shades of night, black and hollow, like he has been dead for years and suddenly he was awakened. His long, spidery hair flies wildly from the two hundred mile an hour wind, yet he stands firm in his storm. Yes his storm, a storm that should be well below thirty-six thousand feet. Heavy rains have him soaked to the gills, yet he pays no mind. He just stares at John, absorbing his fear, then turning his back to him and looks out into the darkness on the edge of the wing, absorbing the visage of a dark and stormy world. The black rags he wears fly in the wind like a war torn battle flag whipping from the high, wet winds.

John feels a tugging on his shoulder. He screams as he turns to see a stewardess. "Please sir, you must buckle your seat belt" Said with a strong, Dutch accent, not paying attention to John's pansy shriek. They were distant words coming from her; the focus of her thought was on the top of the cabin, hearing something like boulders hitting the outside. Her eyes focused upward as she disappears into the darkness of the plane. She knows something is wrong, the fear on her face that is shared by all on this flight explains everything.

A flash across the window has his attention once more, John glares out in the darkness of the night sky. Flicker is by the closest turbine to the fuselage and grinning. He can see him clearly from the green glow that illuminates the deep cracks of his face. A deep green emanates from him and the more he grins, the deeper the glow. His spider-webbed hair is a nest of fireflies with the little creatures zooming in and out of the tangled mess. John looks into the dark, hollow eyes and sees the flies twirling and illuminating the sockets of Flicker's skull. The fabric on his body flails wildly from the winds, torn shreds of blackness, clinging to a green-faced monster that owns this stormy night and the destiny of flight 642!

John's heart is in his throat as he watches in horror the dramatic end unfolding before his eyes. This child of the dead was about to lavishly write the destiny of John Roth and the rest of flight 642. His skin crawls with chills, knowing that its midnight over the dark, deep Atlantic Ocean and the thought of becoming fish food is disturbing.

The beast outside the window begins twirling his head slowly, like in some sort of trance, suddenly snapping it forward, peering into John's eyes. Giving a little shirk, he curtsied in a polite, dignified, disturbing manner, and in a flash of lightening, with evil melting over his face he jumps into the air and disappears from John's sight over the fuselage. Looking out, trying to look up, but sees nothing except storm clouds twirling violently. The plane begins to vibrate—dropping what seems ten to twenty feet at a time. Shaking and vibrating with the lights of the cabin suddenly going black! The airflow has stopped with a dark suffocation engulfing him. John feels through the dark—feeling the seat in front of him, trembling, he touches the rough fabric, feeling brittle and old, swearing it was the lid of his coffin. Inside the cabin is shear blackness. The wind and rain is pounding the air liner with the force of a hammer, making it bounce like an old truck on pot-holed dirt road. The only light now is the repeating, sporadic flash of lightening from the outside. Like a flash bulb going off in a dark room, the passengers eyes were wide with terror, staring straight into nothing, into the flash of their lives, waiting for it to be over— waiting for the end! Even in this camaraderie of terror, this group of lost souls, John was alone. Sitting in silence, fully understanding what was happening and why.

Little spots of green started to fill the darkness. Green tints here and there were consuming the cabin multiplying quickly. Little flashes in front of him and in the distance—they were fireflies at thirty-six thousand feet! As John sat in the dark, his eyes swimming back and forth in a sea of darkness trying to catch a ray of light, a sensation came over him. There is an overwhelming feeling of a new presence in the aircraft. A dark feeling, crawling up his spine as the planes engines begin to throb through John's body. He is soaked with sweat as though he was out on the wing in the horrid night himself. Suddenly a feeling came over him, he swallowed hard, he knew the bastard that killed his brother and the others is now here, somewhere in the cabin. He focused long and hard in the darkness of the craft, waiting for the flash from the storm he would look hard, and finally it showed itself. There, in the distance something began to glow. Slowly pulsing and taking form—like a thinly spread, green fog pulling together. The face of a long dead child in a monsters body began to solidify, the blurry face already smiling from the screams that echo the fuselage as its grotesque body comes into focus. The terror is his energy; the lifeblood of his being is absorbed from the horrified people surrounding him. The water dripped off him like a mischievous child caught playing in a murky puddle. His hair now matted to his head, with his chest heaving as he started to move down the isle, absorbing everyone's fear with joy. There was no movement of his legs. They seemed mangled or seriously disfigured, hanging like dead fish dangling the air. He floats in a green haze that surrounds him with the lightning bugs swarming through the cabin; it was the only lighting on the plane except for the sporadic flashes of lightning coming from the storm. An old woman sobbing profusely fell to his feet, grabbing his fishlike sodden legs, begging for mercy. Under her eyes were black tears mixing with mascara that painted her cheeks, looking up at this demon for some sort of salvation.

"Please don't hurt us! Please have mercy!" Flicker's face softened, petting the woman lightly on her gray nest of hair. "I won't hurt you, my dear." Said with a smile, he petted some more, he started to hum what seemed to be a lullaby. However the compassion he showed melted away as he glanced over at John. His face distorted, he began grinding his teeth, you can hear them crack and splinter with burning anger. He picked her up by the neck, twisting her sobbing face towards John, "He is the one who will hurt you! Just see what he did to me! Look at me!" Though her eyes were wide with terror, she could not look at the demon before her. She was too busy gurgling for air in his tight grip. Fire Flies were bouncing off her face, in and out of her mouth, making her gag even more. Turning to John he threw her aside like an old doll, blood stained the fuselage from her impact. A big man in a bad suite came from nowhere, attacking him, with a forefinger to one side of his temple the attack was over as quick as it started. The finger went knuckle deep with a wet, slurping sound into the side of his skull. As the man fell, a horrible sound was heard as the wet, sinew-dripping finger slipped from the open wound. Licking his finger, floating over the dead man, he moved down the aisle. This is all happening in a green haze of the jetliner with lightning bugs blinking and tormenting through the darkness. All lighting of the craft is out. What seemed like lightening was the sparks flashing outside the windows from the smoldering turbines. They all were going to die.

Flicker drifted in his green haze, like headlights in the fog coming at you on a dark road on a balmy night. John can see the fire flies swirling in the black sockets of his eyes. The soaking wet rags that cling to his body glisten with a jade tint from the green haze swirling around him. Drifting down the aisle a demon possessed, riding the colored cloud like a magic carpet coming straight for John.

John sat there glued to the chair with eyes wide with searing terror as the fire flies swarmed his face. As annoying as they were bouncing off his face, he can't move, can't even lift a hand to swat them away. Now floating over him like a nightmare is Flicker, his face bent with a grin, feeling the anguish pouring out of John. "Long time no torment, John."

"I—I had nothing—"

"SHUT YOUR MOUTH!"

Grabbing his throat, John's air is immediately cut off. Flickers hand felt like wet, saturated, autumn leaves around his neck. He squeezes the blood to John's head with such delight, feeling the pulse of the troubled turbines through John's neck. Pulsing and gasping, it's hard to distinguish between them both—but nonetheless it gives him pleasure. The red face now with a tint of purple and bulging white eyes beam with terror at his executioner! To Flicker, this is not murder, this is a symphony, his symphony—a concerto of sweet music—an opera being played out by the protagonist named of John Roth. Flicker's face was sweet with pleasure. As the music played through his hand, he was interrupted by a sudden, jolting shock. John felt this through Flickers tight grip, bringing him back from a fading land of pleasure. Again another, and John could see the cause of the electrical charge through his returning eyes. The burning hair stiffened his senses as he fell back into his seat being let loose from the slimy hold. Flickers face was now white with anger. He turned to find one of the pilots holding a stun gun. Fear hit him like a cold wind. He stood frozen as the lightning bugs began to multiply on his face. More and more were swarming him like flies on shit; it was irritating to watch the little things crawling up and down his face and neck, in his ears and mouth as it hung wide with fear, illuminating like a Christmas tree in a green fog. Flicker grabbed his throat, crushing the bugs that were crawling there and grabbing the stun gun in a movement unknown to any human. He looked at it with a strange curiosity, pulling the trigger and watching the beam of electricity flow across its insect-like antenna, touching the flow with his long, grotesque tongue in subtle amusement. A long, slimy trail of saliva stretched from the pulsing current, Flicker twirled his tongue with delight as the puss-stretched mucus stretched like a spider's web being spun.

"Lets turn it up a bit, shall we?"

The poor mans face and body are almost all covered in green, flickering bugs, crawling the torsion of his face, except where a dead hand wrapped his neck. Flicker held the stinger tight in his hand; with a wink to his victim, he jammed it in his mouth. A gust of evil charged the gun more than it was meant to withstand. The copilot was jerking and shaking with a strange, green current flowing through him. The lightning bugs began to glow a steady green all at once, brighter and brighter as the evil current ran through his convulsing body. Flickers arm was smoking and shaking with the man's feet kicking out from under him. Finally he let him go, dropping to the floor of the cabin, quivering, covered with crawling fire flies. Shaking violently for a moment, then it all ended, he is dead. The bugs began to take air once more, slowly filling the cabin.

"That's it!" "I had enough of these petty games!"

Something once called Tom Flicker stepped on the dead mans head, then leaping to the top of the cabin. He looked like a slimy serpent clung to the ceiling, looking over the soon to be dead souls of the plane. A hideous grin melted over his face and in an instant, he was heading to the front of the plane like a fast moving lizard.

John sat there in the flickering dark, not knowing what to expect, not knowing what to do. He is lost in the misery of what's happening. The screams were becoming too much for him, tears rolled in his eyes. Besides the hysteria happening around him, he hears the most horrifying sounds coming from up front in the cockpit, yet he can't move. He feels the plane twist with a thump through his legs. Dim lights began to illuminate the cabin. There, in a few rows up, a little girl is turned, staring at John. With all the chaos going on, they just look at each other. Her eyes were flowing with sorrow as the lightning bugs danced around her face. The sweaty hair wrapped her hazel eyes, her lips trembling, she just looked at John. She reminded him of the doll you always saw scorched and burned in the bombed out buildings of the old world war two flicks. It was hard for him to look at her, look into the wide, innocent eyes. But he forced himself:

"This isn't my fault," he cried, but the hurting engines flooded any sound John could muster.

He couldn't look; he began to sob, covering his face.

"Turn the hell around!" John screamed into the whine of the turbines. She couldn't hear him, but she knew what he meant. With a sudden jerk, she was lost behind the seat. He was relieved; looking into the eyes of Flicker was easier than an innocent child. Swatting away the bugs gathering, he laughed. The eyes of innocence are burning John's conscience. He laughed at the thought of a little girl killing him long before Flicker had his chance.

Then it started...

John realized there was a bright red glow coming from the window. When he looked out, the wing was ablaze, splintering and peeling away, with little fireballs bouncing off John's window. Chuckling in hysteria, he buckled up...

A sudden burst from the engine, the wing began folding and the fuselage started to roll into it. The huge 747 started to twist and turn in the sky thirty-six thousand feet up. John was lost in vertigo, feeling a constant drop in his stomach. He felt drops of water hitting him but he can't see because of the black, billowing smoke of burning fabric filling his lungs. His eyes are shut tight, but he still feels the sting from the thick, blanket of black poison engulfing him. The thick smoke has eaten John's air. He doesn't believe this is happening, but he knows it's real because now he can feel the rain. When we dream we are falling, we always wake before we hit. Not this time. This nightmare will be his last; he knows he will not awake from this nightmare because he can feel the rain. The fuel tanks erupt and the only thing left is a fireball streaking through the night sky.

It's morning. Flight LKM 642 laid spread out in pieces on the ocean surface, with the bulk of it lost at the bottom of the Atlantic. The fog is thick and the rescue party is lost in it some where far away. Bodies and pieces of bodies and debris float sporadically in the murky, black water—a purgatory of the dead. The fuel fires that scorched the surface are starting to die. The sound of a helicopter is off in the distance but it too is lost in the fog searching for the wreckage. A piece of the fuselage bobs up and down as a fragmented, raft. And on it, stands the demon that caused all this destruction. Looking out over the debris, kicking a sneaker out of his way, he seems relaxed now. All the bastards that made him what he is are dead and now he can sleep. He begins to bend, heaving his chest; a green haze floats out of the shell of this monster. It slowly drifts through the fog and disappears in the thick of it. What's left of his body turns to ash and crumbles away.

Tom Flicker is truly gone.

John awakes to a white light. It's off in the distance and he is slowly going towards it. He feels the warmth and serenity coming from the light and he wants to go. However something is holding him back. He tries to pull away from what ever has a hold on him, but it's futile, he can't pull from this invisible grip. The frustration builds and a steady flow of anger starts to engulf him. The light begins to fade with John's eyes filling up with tears. To his shock, he coughs up water, dirty, filthy water coming from his lungs. This shocks him as he gets pulled from the warmth, again, he vomits—it drifts the waters in front of him, it's hard to breath; he gasps for air in between fits of gushing water coming from inside him. Everything is blurry and begins to liquefy—he begins struggling in the cold, murky water. Tasting the fuel of an airliner, his stomach turns with nausea. Looking up, he sees a wavy face looking down at him, with an arm breaking the surface of the water, a hand from the reflection pulls John's head out of the oil-patched mess. He shakes the oil from his eyes and coughs up dirty, salty tasting oil out of his mouth. He looks in horror as the water drains from his eyes. He realizes his brother Keith is pulling him from his would be watery grave. "Hello, little brother. We have much work to do." It's the old gang, standing on a floating wing. And fat boy is there, staring at the dawn of a new day, rubbing his swollen jaw. "You can run Flicker, but you can't hide!"

Maɔman in the Moonlight

A cool breeze caresses my face with the fragrances of a thousand worlds filling my nose. Lifting my lids is hard to do—yet I force them wide for the mysterious delirium that is lavishly beginning to unfold before me. Raising my head, I am light as a feather. Hearing the sounds of a fit, I roll over in mid air and see myself convulsing wildly on my bed, twitching and jerking while something of myself (I can't explain) floats peacefully above my body. "Oh, yes, it's me," muttering aloud with an unconcerned and piteous thought, I'm sure this is supposed to be the end, yes, the end of me. But it's not over—at least not yet, not for me…

It's so hard to look at myself lying there when all I see is a carcass of misery. However foul as it is to see, it's not why I'm here now. It's to see something of the end, I know this must be a dream, or, some sort of vision, but why I am brought here, I don't know— yes this is my room, the floor, the furniture, however the walls and ceiling are gone giving way to a shimmering star-filled cosmos!

The stars that fill these heavens glisten like emeralds of reddish blue fire burning outward through the atmosphere into an endless, dark unknown. It's so beautiful watching the deep sky loom with nebulas and pulsars ever in motion with a large Magellan cloud being my focus of intent and awe. Shooting stars stream and trail across the night sky like fireworks on a steamy, hot Fourth of July night. Everything here beams with life, swimming and swirl-ing as far as the naked eye can see. But the night sky is only one enigma of this world; a deeper ambiguity engulfs my surroundings. Worlds within worlds are all around me, floating, waiting for my intent curiosity to touch their unearthly unknown.

Windows of all shapes, sizes and designs are haphazardly adrift in sporadic spots throughout this place. Hundreds and hundreds just silently sway in a cosmic mist of this strange and beautiful world that once was my room. Old, broken panes protrude from rotten, wooden frames. Sills covered in dust and dirt suspend in an aura of some long past misery. Others are aloft high with glints of soft, lavender rays falling from their ridges covering the other win-dows that lay well below. I see these windows, and I see the other worlds that touch their glass. I see the life that exists on the other side of these panes. Every floating window here reflects its inner world outward to this one, casting some distant reality of colors and sounds—blending together in what was once my room.

I myself am transparent, almost glass-like. I can see clear through my hand without the structure of bones, veins or blood but clear and surprisingly flexible. I am dressed in a suit of white clouds that move and whirl in a sea of blue haze. I know from past ventures that these clouds are harmonious with my mind, drifting wonderfully through my transparent structure, ever in motion with the wavelength of my thoughts. The body that lay behind me is a dreadful carcass, spoiled by disease, slowly withering away.

Sleeping tumors lay dormant, waiting silently to awaken and consume the internal organs until you can no longer function as an independent individual. For months after the butcher's knife, you are engulfed in horrific pain that casts out the last ounce of hope you once grasped so dearly. Then they administer the opium: Your delightful, death sentence. You become a stoic, staring slab waiting to fade away from your relative's uncaring memories.

"I know."

"I've seen this before through a child's eyes."

However, because of this place, my outlook has differed. The carcass, I've come to understand, is just a holding tank of the miseries of my world. Guilt with gravity weigh heavily on our shoulders, pushing us down into a deep, deep, depression, limited by the boundaries of the body itself.

But for now, lets move on to brighter things.

Knowing my time is short I float by and only glance at these different panes of other worlds clinging in the air. I slice in between, over and under, around, pushing windows gently out of my way, to get to this one window further back of my endless room. Getting closer, I can hear showers of water hitting the glass of my preferred destination: The window of rain.

"Splitter, splatter," fills my good ear. As I approach this sill, lightening flashes, thunder rumbles, and my suit of clouds twists and turns with excitement. This window is shaped like a giant teardrop about six feet high and four foot wide in its middle. Individual frames crisscross its center, making it look like an oval, chessboard, standing on end. The old curtains that hang, and the sill itself are saturated with moisture and mildew, beads of water are dancing and multiplying on the glass from the constant battery of heavy rains penetrating the rotting wood that's losing the battle against the elements and it's ally—time...

It has been raining here a long, long, time and it's beautiful! Melting waves of water drip and waggle over and down the glass in an unparalleled synchronicity. Touching the pane, I can feel the chill of another world through my empty glass like hand. Strange, incandescent lights protrude a dark shadowy outline of a castle-like structure illuminate other windows out there. My soul flares with excitement, as my glass eyes become focused on an oriole that is across and just below my window.

"Huh! There she is." Muttering low through my lips, a silhouette of beauty touches the pane, reflecting her enigma back into my eyes. Through the rain, I see her. She's sheltered in swirls of shadows of a blue abyss, swallowed and pampered by the warm, low, lights of her dwelling. Her hair is long and amber, touching her white gown that surely (even though it's hard to see) touches the floor.

A Flash— then a rumble.

In this burst of light, I see her fully, a silhouette solidified with her picture permanently blazoned in my mind. However sadly, it fades hollow as the flash goes out, fading to shadow. In that instant her beauty roared in my eyes, as the rains fall, pouring down through a howling wind, beating the ground, releasing the misty soul of her world to float high with the cirrus of that strange universe.

Again, a flash—then a crack!

Once more her aura flared to bright velvet, and sadly, suddenly, it melted back to an outlined darkness. The candles' light floating her room cushions her gentle movements, bouncing her shadow from wall to wall as she moves to the window of her strange dwelling. She absorbs the heavy rains falling before her like a black rose swaying in a storm. Her face is a blur from the water pouring down the glass, but somehow, I know she is beautiful. She looks on, scanning the horizon until suddenly her head turns, snapping in my direction. She is staring at my window and me. I feel the grip of her eyes locking onto me. Her body stiffened, staring at this horrible invader looking down onto her world.

A flash—and a boom!

In that flash, I can see her eyes wide, black almonds absorbing and swallowing my soul. There is a joining of us, or, some sort of take over. She holds me tight in her vision, I can't move. I am pulled closer to the window, Lifted off my heels with my face smearing the already dirty glass. It seems she wants a better view of her intruder. I can feel my darkest secrets and fears being peeled away and devoured by her. Then with a sudden, gentle jerk of this creature's head, I am free. The bond is broken, and I drop back on my heels. In that instant, she steps back, still staring at me like a wild animal watching her prey. Suddenly she turns to zigzag through strange obstacles, disappearing into the black of her room.

Flash, crack, flash - KaBoooommm!

Everything is bright, black, bright, then black again. Opening my glass eyes, I am on the ground, the window exploded and the storm that was once divided by glass now is raging wildly, uncontrollably, throughout my room. The rains are pouring in, the windows that hung the air, are being sucked out; a phenomenon I can barely explain. Everything is shifting back and forth, back and forth, my glass hand is starting to crack and splinter into tiny shards and fall away. My suit of clouds is violently, bristling, across my chest and exiting all the cracks that started to form over my glass body; like an old boiler, letting off steam, ready to explode. A fog coiled outside my body and I know now, that I am leaving—the dream, this wonderful dream is fading...

Shades of darkness begin to cradle me, releasing the anxiety and excitement that have built up in my temporary housing of glass. Silence is here, I know it is—but I cannot hear it. The humming is coming back, crawling up my spine, louder, and louder, until it floods my right ear once more. The glass of illusion breaks and reality fills my eyes. I have awakened from a beautiful dream—I have awakened in total disappointment....

* * *

Again, I'm awakened from my slumber! The explosion in my head and ringing in my ear makes my life a sleepless hell! When I do manage to drift, the anguish above erodes my dreams, turning them into nightmares that erupt in my mind! For eleven long years I have tolerated the pain, but this ringing! "Oh, this horrible ringing!" a constant hum echoing throughout the inner canal of my ear! I wake in pools of sweat from a malicious phantom that engulfs my body! I can tolerate the menacing bastard during the day as I go about my daily business, but when day creeps into the night, casting shadows of mayhem and illusion, flooding the streets of the iron bound section of this pit called Mirrors, he is there, around every corner, screaming in my ear. Why dear God has he picked me!

There's no beauty in this lost, lowly, polluted world, just hundreds of stone laid roads lined by dark, sullen factories dimly lit by street lamps filled with the oils of dead whales, congesting the already foul air with the stench of an unnecessary slaying. Not to mention the lonely drunkards and whores looking for affection in the arms of disease ridden lovers. They live in a whirlpool of intoxicating dissolution and are blind to the reality around them. "Poor them!"

At least they have an excuse, I am the one loosing the boundaries of reality and no booze has passed my lips ever! I have smelled opium only from a distance after passing the many dens that lay hidden in the cracks of society, never indulging and yet, I am the one going mad!

Late at night, with sleepless, mad eyes I stare off into the darkness of my bedroom. The quiet is horribly loud, the humming in my right ear even louder. The phantom begins his nightly wailing in my mind. He begins tormenting the last of my sanity! Staring up at the ceiling, it begins to change from a solid form to a moving, melting violent sea of white. Perspiration pours from my body as phlegm crawls in my throat. My heart pounds the inner shell of my chest, the mattress I claw for dear life! My ear begins to bleed; blood and puss run the nape of my neck as tears fill my eyes! "No more" every night he distorts my inner eye and makes my outer world a living hell! "No More" came from deep inside me. It was so distant, so far away that I almost answered myself. "No More" came the cry again, this time my lips mimicked the lovely words that were deep in my body. Syllables of serenity flew from my lips repeatedly. "No More, No More!" Tonight his life will come to an end! No longer will I allow this venom to stream through my veins. I will not tolerate his world any longer!

"IT ENDS!" Vertigo has me housed in a womb of paranoia, but I say it all ends—tonight!

Sitting up, I move to the edge of my queen size bed, that's fit for a king. Gently I rest my feet on a beautiful, hand made Oriental rug. Woven colors of gold and silver are separated by black wool interweaving the main color combination to bring out its wonderful design. Only to be enhanced by a five-tear chandelier that glitters soft diamonds hung from finished oak beams that crisscross the archway of my ceiling. Cascading spectacles of light flow through my room with a timeless and somewhat mystical glow—spinning and dancing through the air that I, will soon, no longer breathe.

I watch the soothing shimmers of tiny lights amalgamate then climb the French-made olive colored curtains that fall to the floor. All around me it looks like glowing snow, swirling from an invisible, non-existing wind. Long departed relatives stare, with what seems endless torment, or jealousy, out of glass frames on my bedroom walls. Often I thought it could be the howl of their hatred that thrusts and boils uncontrollably in my head. After all, they would sell their soul for such a gift, but nonetheless, an exorcism will take place tonight and I will win!

A marble fireplace blesses this chamber with a lovely smell of cedar, filling my senses and kicking in memories of days long past. Above this expensive pit of warmth and flames is suspended the most precious painting I own. The colors illuminating my chamber flicker and float across her cheek. Lorelei Luray. Madness took her and now the beast is after me.

After a moment of thought, turning without hesitation, wiping my eyes, I turn to the garden doors that are adjacent to my bedroom. However before I get half way there the winds of October blew them wide, stopping me dead in my tracks! A boisterous blast sends the French drapes and what's left of my thinning hair into a spastic twirl. My vision locks on the dark, October air that now fills my lungs and waters my eyes with images of fear of what's waiting for me out there. It surely seems that nature herself has agreed with my decision!

Moving out onto a balcony of moss-covered stone, stopping at the edge I look down onto a magnificent garden. The design is my own to escape the chaos and disorder of this lost, lowly world.

Its beauty is reflected by a large harvest moon, swimming through a sea of stars. The songs of midnight play soothingly in twilight, flowing softly on one side of my head, blending with a horrible hum in the other, yet I can't help swaying to the tranquil music of nature.

Standing at the edge of stone stairs, I grab one of the lanterns that are atop a lion's head, which is the beginning of a long journey down an ivy-covered stone railing. A low rumble from the south turns my head to that corner of the sky. "A storm is coming". Black clouds paint the heavens with a dull disorienting visage. "Very strange for October" floats through my head while opening a little compartment under the lamp's base and pulling out a waxed-soaked match. Striking it on the lion's head, it flares to life. Quivering I rest it against the wick and slowly the smell of a dead whale inflames my nostrils. Having no choice but to breathe its murder, I lower the glass. The aura of this poor creature's lost soul begins to glow through the chilly night of my garden. The thunder grows louder and the wind harsher with lightning flashing a bluish-green not white—this is indeed strange for October. But no matter, the outside world does not concern me anymore. My personal dream and creation awaits me; the final walk though my garden.

A pathway of tiny, white, stones lay before me. I always loved that crunching sound they made while walking through my tranquil paradise. The moon flowers of autumn wildly dance on a trellis running then disappearing into the darkness of my lush, living, green maze; Only blooming at night, by the mystical moons light, it was a must that they take root, and flourish in my obscure world.

The dwarf Japanese maples cluster together on one side looking very eerie, casting ghost-like shadows that run frantically through the dense night as I pass with the lanterns wicked glow. The shadows are like the souls of lost children playing in the trees, jumping chaotically from limb to limb then leaping high into the blackness above, now free, disappearing into the ethos of the night sky. How wonderful it must be to dance in heaven!

An eight-foot wall stands with thick, green hemlock's, surrounding the outer perimeter of my garden, protecting my privacy from probing eye's stealing the curiosities of my private creation. But I guess now it really doesn't matter anymore. All that I accumulated over the years out of greed and avarice is all crumbling away; it all means nothing in the end, just a dark, lonely soul looking for some sort of salvation in a world that has gone incredibly mad.

Now the rains start to fall heavily on my face. Beads of icy drops send chills through my body making me quiver. Poetic wonders would ooze freely through me every time I walk in my garden, but now, even here, I can't escape the perils of vertigo. His torment walk's hand in hand with my soul, and there's nothing, as a living man, I can do about it!

A faint sound catches my ear, a low howl riding a soft breeze from the nearby ocean, or is it the woods lining both sides of my gate, stretching as far as the eye can see, disappearing into the black of night. With the angry tides crashing the battered cliffs and the constant hum in my head, it's hard determining the exact location of the drifting, soft sound. There is an odor of unease drifting the wind and with a slight case of paranoia, I move on.

The white stones now glow yellow from the cold rains; they end at a six-foot high, by four-foot gate. Dank and dingy, it hasn't been passed through in years. Oh, how it creaked and moaned, but the rust deposits were no match for the strength of my curiosity and my determination to open it.

Now standing outside my haven, the turbulence of the sea talks too me in ways it has never done before. I absorb the lovely sounds that sing from just over and below a distant cliff some hundred or so yards away. Yes, voices of the sea ride the strong wind coming from the oceans below, harmonically soothing my troubled mind. Fields of tiger lilies sway in the wind all around me, absorbing the light rain falling upon them. They glide in an eerie unison, sliding side to side, pushed by nature's harsh wisdom. How hypnotically rhythmic they are in a world so out of balance. I touch the cup of a lily next to me, soft, wet with dew, how beautiful it is to watch the rest dip and sway in the dead of night.

A frost of a howl chilled my spine once more echoing a disturbing shiver throughout my body. It lay long through my head as the hair on my neck slowly rose bewilderingly frigid. "It's coming from the woods." Saying to the lilies, not expecting a response of course but out of a spontaneous reaction of fear the words slip from my mouth falling dead on their wind drifting motion. The dark wilderness is erupting violently with nocturnal activity, the scampering of many things move through the foliage that lies under the dark canopy. However suddenly, except for the ocean, everything went quiet.

After the long silence, low growls began filtering through the shrubbery. What I thought were lightning bugs going about their business—were not! Eyes of fire glow softly from the woods, with forming shadows around the amber's that swim in the darkness. The whip of willows beat an old log; the war drum sounds, or is that my heart? Another growl, following with a long howl echoed through the night, not to mention my spine. The shadows begin to solidify. "I can see what they are" whispering to the lilies, "They're jackals" I read about them in old Egyptian texts, when you die, the jackals come from the shadows and lead your soul to the underworld. An old ancient myth I thought, but here they are, swarming like bees on honey. They form a line behind me. I should have run to the gate but I cannot move. Nor do I have any plans of retrogressing. In the dead night I am still, not moving, fighting the urge to turn my head to see what they are doing. I can feel them, I can feel the presence of these strange creatures and somehow, somehow I know they are not part of the living world, and the horrible odor that wreaks the air tells me they are real. Out of the corner of my eye, I can see their shadow's disturbing the night with alarming movements and whimpers. I feel the burning from their eyes on my back, with low muffled growls vibrating the air. One of these creatures moves out in front of me. He only has one eye of fire with the other long burned out. The side of its skull is shredded and matted with puss, dripping out of a dark, hollow socket. Gnats harass the irritated jackal's rotten sinew that dangles from his cheek, still he stands triumphantly, sniffing the air that my paranoia floats on, absorbing my fear, devouring it, as he would me if I make any wrong move. So I move in the only, obvious way they want me to go, towards the cliffs.

Breaking the flow of innocence, we trample a path through the tiger lilies unity with nature, disrupting their balance so I can fulfill my destiny. I walk what seems forever, following closely by one eye and whirled in a penumbra by countless others, being pushed towards the mountain overlooking the ocean.

Now I stand at the edge staring into an empty void of a black sea. The waves crash white against the jagged rocks far below, thrusting and foaming then melting back into the dark waters. The chilly rains penetrate my clothes and now I begin to shiver, while the clouds above swirl in a distorting havoc throughout the night sky.

"What a wonderful night to die – wouldn't you say?" Lightning flashed and lit the sky like an annoying flash bulb, illuminating the infectious beasts that surround me. I can't stand to look at them as the thunder rolls away their whimpers from the bright flash swelling their eyes. The light only seemed to Anger them, making them irritably impatient for me to finish my task. Growls and snarls push me back—a fence of hideous hounds has me at the edge of my death step with my back to the bleak sky!

My ear begins to ring, louder and louder I am loosing balance on all grounds! The carcasses that surround me melt to shadows and suddenly five darting streaks begin violently erupting around me. Their hideous sounds fill the air as they move in and out of a penumbra, swirling around me like a mysterious dust storm! Then the reality of my dilemma sinks deep into my hand. The ripping and tearing of flesh sends a hammer of pain up my arm! Cries to heaven went unanswered, drowned by this creature's pleasure of ripping fingers from my hand! I step back in agony, clenching what is left, fingers gone, ripples of blood pour from the wound, sending my mind in utter confusion. "This must be a dream!" Howls and humming fill my head and I dance with laughter at the edge of the cliff. Flinging my hand back and forth the warm blood splatters my cheek and I laugh! The heavens open above and a bright light shines down on me and I dance! I feel the edge of the cliff give way under foot and I dance and I laugh! The blood is warm and I am so very tired, and I laugh! Soon I will dance in the mists of other worlds, but still here I dance, and in the bright light I...AAAAAHHHHHHH!!!!!!!

* * *

Bubbles...

All I see are blurred bubbles...

Something is pulling me deep into a dark, mysterious abyss. A tide pulls me down as I watch the bubbles of air escape my water filling lungs. They swirl to a blurry surface of light that is getting smaller as I sink deeper. Little beads of air roll off my cheek, the softness of the flow is beautiful, still sinking deep into silence, a calm I never felt before, where blackness echoes nothing, just a soothing silence telling me that it is finally, finally over.

The caress of a warm light touches my face, forcing me to open my eyes in my watery tomb. This light drifts on the currents in the distance and its origin is far above me. I seem to be rising now instead of sinking. It grows in dimension as I slowly rise towards its radiance. The waters push me up through the fathoms to its warmth. Its pulsing, growing wider and wider with the liquid engulfing me begins to dissipated. I can't see anything around me, it is so bright. Suddenly, the brightness slowly fades, and a white hue starts to take shape, molding and forming to a silhouette like a desert mirage weaving in the heat of a noontime sun. The wreathing stopped, and a familiar world begins to solidify around me with colors filling the whiteness, blooming into reality. Images of the cliff where I fell are starting to emerge. Yes, it's the edge all right, what happened to the storm, and the jackals? My clothes are still shredded and my skin is so very pale. My hand! It's healed! "One, two, three, four, five fingers!" they're all there. I count again and again, all five fingers! What is happening? I thought I was dying but somehow I survived. And now I feel wonderful! It's a beautiful night! Even though it is dark the world seems so bright to me now. The stars are huge and oh so many! Did the waters cure me? I don't feel dead. Knotting my fingers with curiosity the questions ran though my mind over and over. The rains have surrendered with a harvest moon lighting the night in a pool of soft, mollifying, nighttime blue. The sea glows an emerald green with the light of a rainbow glowing through the dark and touching its waters; it's the most amazing thing I have ever seen!

The music of this new world beats beautifully on both eardrums and the horrible humming that tortured me all those years is gone.

And with the-

"Good God what is that!"

Off in the distance, in the far corner touching the horizon something is erupting. The shock of an explosion smacked me, jolting me, almost knocking me over. Red, amber and orange fire with flaring projectiles fill the distant sky, letting go of black, smoldering, clouds visible by the moon's illuminating glow. Something horrible is happening. I can feel it deep in my body, but I'm not afraid. Something inside me tells this is inevitable, it's all right, this must happen and it will happen.

I turn towards where my garden's gate once stood; the shrubs and the rooftop of my house are gone. All I see are miles and miles of lilies dancing in the wind, bending back and forth in a rhythmic unison on beams of light projecting from a distant corner of this world.

I turn my head, dumfounded by what I see, before me stands a ladder!

"God Damn!" I shouted, and with that moment thunder roared the second I finished those words, though swallowing my tongue seemed to ease the rumble's above, cringing from the gods, I glanced up and say, "But it wasn't there a minute ago."

The ladder is made of cold iron and is very, very rusty, yet with a slippery, dampness to its feel. It curves through the air disappearing high above into white, thick, clouds and by no means is it loose or wobbly. Except for the bowing, it's solidly-sunk deep into the earth. I try shaking it but it doesn't budge; it's planted firmly! It reminds me of a diver's platform at the circus many years ago. After the clown's and elephant's did their show, a man would climb high into the canopy, shrinking to a speck. After a long drum roll and a hush over the crowd, he would leap in the air, growing from a speck to a man, taking forever to finally splash into a tub of water.

Now the same type of ladder stands before me, only this one is much higher than any circus diving platform, this one disappears through the cloud's high above. With stoic thoughts I turn once again to the chaos erupting over the ocean. It's growing bigger; slowly eating its way towards me with the smell of sulfur stinging my nose. It's obvious now that this world is being consumed by evil with fiendish entity's waiting to be unleashed. I hear their moans and the hideous laughter of demons drifting in the hot wind. And it's even more obvious that something I cannot explain wants me to climb this latter to the clouds. I turn once more to see if my garden gate was there, a piece of something to remind me that I belong here, but there is nothing. So onto a new mystery that stretches to the sky. A burning wind came suddenly; for some reason it didn't affect me, but the lilies now lay dead on their sides. Miles of lilies instantly turned brown and fell over. It look's as if most of the heat is coming from the ground, bubbling like a kettle of tar, turning, smoking and rippling under foot. Strange looking mushrooms are popping from the earth growing to the size of pumpkin's instantly in front of me, ugly brown things tainted with greenish, blackish, spots, things I've never seen before. Yes, it is time to go. And the only way out, undoubtedly, is up!

The ladder is frigid to the touch, not too cold but strangely colder than the new atmosphere that is heating this world. Odors of the dreaded fungus fills the air, "good God the smell is horrible" realizing that I stepped on some of the ugly little things, I've smelled broken mushrooms before but this is intensified twentyfold, and almost brings me to vomit. Shaking my head of the horrible stench, I begin my climb. After cleaning my foot on the first step, I raise it to the second, and my second foot, to the third, and so on. As I climb, the idea of never coming back to earth swim's intensely in my mind, though the reality of it all, and the disease that's spreading, tells me soon there won't be a world to come back to.

Random thoughts of a happy childhood flood my mind, not locking on any one point in particular, but a tidal wave of different, happy times long past and almost forgotten. The thought of long lost winter months has its roots planted deep inside me.

In the morning I would wake and rush to a chilly window sill, staring for hours at white trees with black trunks, bending to the new world that formed over night from the heavy snow that fell the night before. Sounds of winters-wind chimes filled my healthy, young ears every time the wind blew and the frost dust would swirl; Ah those were wonderful times, and now it is surely over...

Never again will children awake to a beautiful winter morning. What a horrible thought to know, that when it is too late, when death is near, then, and only then is the zest for living fully understood. We grow from child, to parent, then grandparent so horribly fast, and it's always the latter when the beauty of life would unfold. And some times even then we die miserable. Definitely not me, these last few minutes of my life I am thankful for the wonderful pictures that filled my head before the eruption, and equally disappointed how I let the disease of my inner ear ruin the last twelve year's of my life. Why it's not tormenting me now, I don't know. But soon it will all be over. As much as some strange force is pulling me up to the sky, the poison will soon touch the bottom of this ladder, and I will bend and fall to my death, but nonetheless I will be at rest.

This ladder seems to be shrinking in girth as the sky opens up to a panoramic portrait of a hazy, nighttime blue. High above me the ladder disappears into the bottom of a massive island of cirrus stratus which is stationary, and which I find very odd, considering the wind is blowing quite steadily up here but nonetheless it stands firm, like a majestic iceberg in the sky.

It reminds me of the hayloft of my grandfathers' old barn. A ladder stretched to a little, dark hole in the ceiling, and now, as then, my body rumbles with curiosity.

Cotton balls of white clouds drift silently by. The ones that come close to me, and with having no fear of the height I have reached, I playfully run one hand through them. I can actually feel the softness of their existence, distorting their structure with the touch of my fingers, waving back and forth, sifting them, and watching them gently float away. It's so marvelous up here in the sky. Absorbing the sights of purity, wonderful things are filling my eyes. But something inside tells me another quarter of a mile up this ladder a new world awaits me. I must see it before I plummet like a stone back to earth.

Sound, on the other hand, is another matter. That is what pulled my eyes from the quiet reality around me. "Swoosh, swoosh," came from behind a thick cloud far below, giving way to a bluish-grey speck, growing rapidly as it climbed through the air, not towards me mind you, but towards the lavender world above. "Good God, it's a man!" Or the form of a man, the grayish color of its skin and hideous black, bat-like wings swooshing through the air suggests something else, something horrible. This demon-like creature is not alone; he's being followed, or chased by four shadows, with no form or body structure, just balls of blurring spots zooming to catch their prey.

As hideous as he looks, he should be the hunter, not the hunted. He flew past me heading upwards, the wind from his mighty wings nearly knocked me from the ladder, paying me no mind, looking over his shoulder for his stalkers, aiming for the little trap door where this ladder ends. However, the slow, swooshing draw of his wings made this creature an easy catch. The shadow demons zoom past me, easily mooring their victim against the ladder above, dividing me from my destination.

A storm of shadows engulfs this creature, pulling him back from his obvious sanctuary high above. The flapping of his giant wings taking air made it a temporary stand off, but the dusty silhouettes were too much, slamming him face first, into the ladder over my head. It sounded like the crack of thunder when he hit, shaking my mount violently, my footing slipped, however I still could not take my eyes off the theatrical enigma in the clouds above me. I can feel this creatures struggle and torment vibrating through my hands, and the hate flowing from shadows with no form. Such hideous giggle's and laughter fall from above, I cringe from the horrible sound, but nonetheless I watch a tiring creature's last bit of hope hang by one hand on a ladder, high in the sky. These demon-like shadows continue their torment, zooming in and out of his body, faster and faster, the weakening beast began to wither and curl, victory is soon theirs. His mighty wings that once captured clouds for flight, now lay limp on his back, saturated with exhaustion his head hangs limp, he's finished. His grip finally loosened, he is slipping down the ladder, however with no strength left to sustain him from the evil slowly eating his soul, he lets go. He falls, tumbling towards me, I catch his arm and my hand gets a good, firm grip. In that instant of touching the beast, the Lavender World above roars with anger. The wind picks up instantly sending this creature's wings flapping wildly in a forceful wind, like two war torn flags in the midst of heavy battle.

His arm feels like moss that dried in the hot sun, flaking away in my hand. His whole body, in some way, reeks of evil—it bleeds from his pores like molasses, and in some profound way, I know this, I know he is a demon from hell, but his eyes tell me otherwise. His eyes are the only thing that tells me he was once human. " Helllppp mmeeee!" He said, hideously rolling from his lips, sending a chill up my spine.

"Let him go, let him go," Sadistic whispers came from the shadows that swirl around him.

"He is evil."

"He is bad."

"He is ours!"

(rrrrrrrrrriiiipppppppppp!!!!!!!!!)

In that instant a shadow took form and ripped one of the wings from this creatures back, the sound of a thousand newspapers being torn filled my ears, along with a horrible scream that echoed through the sky, falling long and slow upon the earth. Tears oozed from his eyes that now are rolling back in his head. He is silent now, held only by the grip of my hand—I am losing my hold. A shadow took form again, this time with fangs, and sunk them deep into my arm, as I screamed to the sky, my grip broke and the creature fell towards earth, followed by the shadow's giggling and laughing as they plummet like meteors, with a streak of fire tailing them. A slow, descending wing flutters like a dead, autumn leaf, slipping and turning in the air, disappearing into a cloud. The wind that blew so harshly also died, it is quiet and peaceful once more...

Just below me I see the backs of birds fleeing in one direction away from the ocean. Countless species of birds flap wildly, filling the air with different shrieks, cackles and chirps, attempting an escape from the hell slowly taking over their world. I myself am mesmerized by how fast it's spreading, and soon it will be swallowing this ladder. So I climb, without hesitating, without looking down, I climb for what seems like an eternity.

I pass a piece of torn flesh of a now surely dead creature clinging to one of the rungs of the ladder. It smells pungent, making me sick, but nonetheless I keep going higher and higher through the bright moonlit sky.

Finally coming to the bottom of this peculiar cloud, it shines and glitters like crystals that have formed in a cave, yet my hand can pass right through them. A mirage of some sort—but nonetheless beautiful. Before I go any further, I turn to a world I once knew as home. Now at this level it looks like a giant atlas unfolding under foot. I bow my head and say goodbye to a paradise lost, and then slip into a mist of the clouds.

I am lost in a thick soup—some sort of limbo, swirling around me as if I were in the center of a merry-go-round. My life began passing before my eye's, my birth, and my youth, right to the present. A collage of pictures rolling in the misty cirrus, but I paid it no mind. There is nothing left to see. I just don't care....

My only concerns now are to keep going through this mysterious fog and get through this curtain of cirrus. A few more steps through obscurity and I am through, and yes—it is a diving platform. This isn't a normal platform by any means, it's made of some sort of limestone I think with railing and with four Gargoyles, perched on each corner looking over the edge with horrific eyes, starring on the lost world below.

I stand on top of this like a rooster on top of the old barn. Proud and stern, I stare into a divine world of perfection. With a bright moon glowing, and the matrix of clouds, it reminds me of freshly fallen snow. A valley in a dream-like winter wonderland, yet it is so very warm. The sensation I feel is like the soft touch of silk caressing my face, riding a gentle breeze. I can see across the horizon, many valleys and hills of white, just go on forever. It is difficult to describe, but far off a great wall of clouds stands firm. A huge cirrus stretching from left to right, as far as I can see. It actually has a glow of lavender to it that pulses slowly, in and out like a living creature, with the hue going from light to dark. The magnificent splendors I am seeing, feeling and absorbing are not like anything I have ever seen or felt before. A transformation, was again taking place. Lifting my hand to rub my brow, I swallow a deep sigh, my hand along with the rest of me, is again glass once more. I'm radiating the same soft colors as the wall with lavender hues engulfing me with an incandescent glow. It's no dream this time—reality surrounds me, showing true meaning of life and the beauty of creation, and of a divine power that sired this Heaven. Lost in my curiosity for this place, I barely realize the vibrations coming up through my knees. The platform began to shake and agitate slowly underfoot, I grabbed the railing to balance myself, but nonetheless I know it won't be standing long. The fires below are surely consuming the metal rods at the base of this ladder.

As I stand here waiting, holding my balance, sounds of wind chimes fill the air. Slowly the din wrapped my head, instantly I'm feeling totally relaxed, at ease, forgetting about my soon, baleful demise from plummeting to earth. Now, soft cries are drifting with the chimes—two, very different sounds—yet almost harmonizing together, mesmerizing my thoughts with an almost spellbound chant.

An astounding thing begins to happen; the great wall begins to divide down the middle. It splits with streaming bright rays shooting out like lightning from the inside, beaming colors of purity, exploding to rainbows, illuminating everything around me into a soft cascade of thoughts filling my head with why I'm here, and why I was called.

It's so wonderful to be experiencing this miracle; my eyes feel as wide as the moon above me. In this bliss of revelation, I am caught by a vision off in the distance. As I stand in the warm moonlight, I begin to rise, floating off my perch, as I do it falls from my feet. I watch the platform drop into the clouds, disappearing into the soup of cirrus below me and yet, I am still here, floating in the moonlight. There is a vision off in the distance, something weaving into reality. Before she can fully come into view, I know who she is, it is my lost love. I laugh out loud as I realize she was the one in my dreams. She was gone from reality but she never left my side.

Floating, I land on the cloud next to her; we stare into each other's teary eyes and hold each other saying nothing. Her touch is soft like velvet, she is oh so real. She pulls from me with a sudden jerk, grabbing my hand, leading me to an open view through the clouds. We gazed out into a blue sky. There are angels coming from the ground, hundreds of beautiful souls are coming from the fires below. My love turned to me with her eyes wet with tears, and said:

"Everyone is coming home."
Gazing out into the lovely sight of cherubs and angels, and the wreathing of the moonlight, I know now, I am truly home....

Flight of a Demon

A storm is coming with the wind blowing harshly against my back. Climbing to my loft on the third floor—I shiver. Keys in hand, I unlock the wonders of my world. A personal domain created by its soul proprietor. I, Martin Abercrombie am the architect and creator of this dismal habitat. I open the door to this mystical land of illusion and what do I see but an empty void. Empty as my inner soul, with no compassion, no burning for life, nothingness! I get this feeling every time I return to this lair of "Depression".

Once, a long time ago, after my world came crashing down around me, I went to confession. No I am not catholic and yes I am definitely NOT religious. However, the greed that coerced my veins, I felt I was owed something for the horrible hand I was dealt. How dare they ruin my life, who ever they are!

On my way to the church, I was pondering ways to get back at God for taking all my worldly possessions, money, woman and my flamboyant, wanton lifestyle that I've, over the years, grown a custom to and rightly earned.

In my mind ran deeds of rampaging through the holy place, knocking over anything and anybody that got in my way. Ripping and tearing whatever I could get my little hands on, until I am dragged out by my ankles with the dust of broken, holy enigma's dirtying my hands! Laughing and giggling hideously the whole way to the nut house, with my taste of revenge satisfied!

But that didn't happen.

I couldn't even go in.

Heading to the kitchen, I light the burner on the stove, then grab the teakettle and turn on the faucet. Filling the kettle with the pollutants of the day, I return it to the flame I just lit. Reaching up, I open the cabinet above the stove and remove an herbal tea bag from the only package filling the massive shelf space. From the sink I take an unwashed mug to make ready a cup of "Cure all" to help ease one man's obscurity of a paranoiac lifestyle. I head to the bathroom to purge myself from one's consumption of poisons and bacteria collected from days past. Ten minutes later, after flushing away the torments of the day, I enter the living room to ready the once owned rocking chair (Thanks Auntie) of my great uncle who just recently past through this world.

Moving the rocker towards the sliding glass doors (my view screen of the world.) I remove the green plastic trash bags that uphold my privacy, to prepare for the wonderful musical that's about to begin.

The kettle starts to whistle, I crumble an old newspaper, rap it around the handle (obviously not to burn oneself), take my cup of roots and leaves, returning to the chair of death with tea in hand. I position myself in a comfortable and reposing way—curtain call, its show time.

* * *

Twilight, after a hot and horrible day of screaming lawn mowers and a hundred and twenty degree weather, the storms finally come to cool the scorching Mesa, Arizona streets for which I work and live. Yes, that is what I do now, a landscaper, learned my trade from the four years in one of Arizona's finest institutions.

The clouds begin to roll off the desert plains. Suddenly, across the openness of the sky, a gray wall of massive destruction starts to swell, igniting my imagination of fear and nervousness to the immensity of the storm itself. With the lightning comes a decorative array of lights and flashes to fill the realm of being with a personal, death-defying picture show, followed with the lovely sound of thunder and rain. Playing perfectly together, it's the most relaxing song of nature to one's ear. The tension lifts out of the body to flow upwards like the steam from the scorching Mesa streets. Together this orchestration of creation is letting us know that the imbalance in our heavens flow flawlessly in bliss and harmony—to give us all a wonderful but temporary distortion of time. Thunderous vibrations felt through the chair help massage this landscaper's sun-torched, baked-body. My eyelids grow heavy now as I descend into the land of nod. Drifting and drifting away.

* * *

I see you. Do you see me?

I dream in darkness with the shapes of its reality molding and forming in swirling rotations all around me. After a few moments, the nauseating swirls stop. There is never any kind of structures in my dreams, no furniture, no trees, nothing, just the blackness of a sleeping mind.

I am so relaxed. The dark is pure heaven too me. Every pore on my body absorbs it, taking all my limitations of a human being away to that boring, and I am sure non-existent bright light that all those religious freaks talk about. After all my tension is gone away, I wait. I wait for the scent of my prey, because soon it will be time to hunt.

Oh—there it is.

That little whiff of body odor and fear. Its blend is sweet on the tip of my tongue. Normally you could not smell it on a clean person, but here, in my dream, my nose can't miss it. Usually it's some person, always just one, always alone, there in the blackness of my own little, dark, dreaming world. Always this person is frightened, scared to death.

After all, wouldn't you be?

They are lost in the blackness of someone's dream.

Someone very, very evil.

I am sure they don't see me, but I see them. I smell them, I smell their fear. I watch them breathe with fear, their chest heaves out of control in the darkness as they try to find their way, trying to find some sort of salvation.

However, in my dreams, I can't let that happen.

I move like liquid, unheard. I circle this beauty in the deep darkness of my dream. The dream is mine—she is mine for the taking.

I dream of what I once was, however, I am manifested into

something far more evil. I always sent fear through people, manipulating them to do whatever I wanted. The flesh of others, the actual physical existence of their bodies was mine, and I took full advantage every moment I could. It was all a game, a wonderful game and I was always the winner—always!

And now it is all gone.

All I have left are these wonderful dreams.

I know what it's like to have control over others and their destiny. How it is to rule and control where there is no say on what they can or can't do or how they live. I took great joy in watching the soul of a man crumble before my eyes. The fragile mind of a woman melt away like an ice cube in the hot desert, it filled me with pure ecstasy. All I wanted was their physical reality, their flesh; the mental ramification was not my problem. All they had to do is do whatever I said.

That's all.

Is that too much to ask?

They say there is always a bigger fish—live by the sword die by the sword—what goes around comes around. I thought I was immune, I thought I was the biggest and best fish.

I was wrong.

God seemed to intervene and ruin my world. Oh' sure you could say hiring turncoat drug addicts to push your drugs was the main problem. I slacked. They got busted and sang like little, yellow canaries. However, here, in my dreams, I still rule. I am king. I am God, and just in front of me, is my prey. I pounce, she screams, I pull her head back, exposing the whiteness of her neck, thin and beautiful. I sink my teeth deep into her soft flesh, tearing it like biting into an apple. A charge of excitement shot through me—electrifying. And I—

* * *

"Damn it!"

My leg burned with pain, ripping me from my dream, my wonderful dream. Nodding off with a hot cup of tea in my hand is up there amongst the high ranks of stupidity! However, the impact of that return still has me effervescing. But it's over. Some of it will be forgotten like every other lost and wonderful dream that comes, enhancing my distorted life then disappearing forever.

I head to the kitchen returning the unwashed mug to its rightful home—the sink. Suddenly I feel sick—a nauseating feeling comes over me. I lean over this germ-filled pit of dirty, disgusting dishes. A scorpion came out of the drain, its stinger flying wild. I stare into the running water, losing myself in its steady flow.

I am surrounded, by wooden walls.

My heart pounds so, my head feels hot and ready to explode. Where am I?

I touch the round, wood and start to panic! The faucet, I hear, is still running, only it's much louder than before. I'm moving, sort of flowing, up and down, like you would on a runaway merry-go-round. Looking up, there's a round hole and a metallic sky beyond it. Cold water splashes over the top, making me wet and cold. The hot air leaves my lungs and turns to a smoky mist. Getting up my nerve to look out the hole seems impossible, but I move. Oh my god! I am in a barrel! Every motion I make rocks me back and forth, up and down, spinning around. Cold, dirty water splashes again over the top, flooding my mind with terror! Gathering what little courage I have, I extend my arms to the top of this wooden hell, pulling myself up to peer over the top. I am frozen in fear, devastated by the world around me!

I'm surrounded by water. We're flowing (the barrel and I) in a chaotic manner, down a white river. The waves crash together, like cars driven by drunks, then melting back into its watery grave. The shore of my surrounding is aligned by jagged rocks and man-made stone fences about waist high on both sides. Behind these stone barricades are hundreds of people in yellow raincoats with their hoods drawn over their heads. It's so misty I can just barely see the flesh on their faces. They're laughing and cheering, pointing at me and my misfortune! Why? Why am I the spectacle of such spineless creatures?

The laughter and cheering grew louder in my head. Holding my ears with cold, drenched hands, I look to see where this renegade nightmare is taking me.

"Oh my GOD!"

Fear hits my face like the waves colliding against the barrel. My eyes are wide, as I look on this immense river. Yes, this water rages but no more than a hundred yards away it all ends. No more white water, just gray sky. My legs buckle, I collapse to the bottom of my soon to be wooden tomb. The flow of the water grows louder along with the laughter and cheering. I'm moving faster, yet I still hear their revelry. I'm glued to the bottom of this barrel. I cannot bear to watch my future, or lack thereof. Covering my eyes in my little tomb, once again my heart is pounding in my temples. Up, down, spinning around, faster and faster, I vomit…

And then…

I stopped moving, miraculously. The thrashing back and forth has ended. One of Gods wonderful creations has ceased tormenting my barrel but the motion in my stomach is in an uproar. The world outside is silent. I don't hear the thunder of the waterfall or that horrendous laughter. A warm, soft breeze blows gently into the entrance of my hell, beginning to dry the water, sweat and other internal fluids that left my body. Catching my breath, the pounding in my head begins to ease. The blood in my veins slows to a normal pulse. At the bottom of my wooden hell I lay mangled. Turning my head awkwardly, I look at the entrance of my exit, waiting to see the face of an angel reaching down with her golden hand. She'll lift my soul from this weary body and take me to a place unknown, out past the endless now blue sky. The longest minute of my life expires, yet nothing appears.

Giving up on any type of salvation, I begin to move my numb legs from their awkward position. I attempt to extend my hands against this rigid chamber, in hopes of getting some type of leverage. But my hand slides, splinters penetrating my finger tips. Finally, in a forceful stretch, I manage to grab the end of my exit (or the end of the entrance) pulling myself erect, while cursing my temporary deformity. Legs quivering, I extend past the exit and look down at the bottom to see if a lifeless body remains. The pain in my legs and hands assures me otherwise—I am still alive.

I attempt to fully open my squinting slits of vision. It's difficult. Fear of the unknown and unseen, the other of drying tears and sweat, almost knotting my eyelashes shut. Rubbing away the buildup, a red sun blinds me. The once flowing river is now an empty bed of dirt and debris, dried and cracked, reminding me of an old map leading nowhere.

The people that line the sides are now lifeless. The flesh that stretched over their racks of bones is gone. The yellow raincoats that were filled with souls of spinelessness and dreadful laughter are now black, holding the structure of bones together as the fleshless figures stare slacked jaw from eyeless sockets, into a dried riverbed.

In my barrel, I turn clockwise, from twelve o'clock to six, and now face the end of the world! I'm two feet from what was the beginning of a waterfall, at the end of the beginning of the endless blue! In horror, I flinch and fall backwards, nearly fainting. Tumbling out of my barrel, stomach skyward, I scramble backwards, kicking up dust like a helpless lamb running from a Jewish blessing. But I know no matter what, it has me and I'm locked in its world with nowhere to run!

Twenty or thirty feet from the end of the endless, my breathing eases once more. Staring towards the edge, I watch the barrel, put into motion from my escape, roll to the end—stop for a moment as though saying farewell, then fall in a suicidal manner. Not once do I hear it hit any obstacles on the way down or it smashing onto the rocks below. It just fell into silence.

Staggering to my feet, my nose begins to run red and wild like the once rapid river. It pours down my face, over my lips, into my mouth, making breathing difficult. While attempting to contain this fluid, the ground underneath me begins to rumble.

"What now!" I shout, as the shaking fills my body, making it nearly impossible to sustain any form of balance. The air is suddenly filled with a screeching sound. Covering my ears, forgetting my nose, I look up towards my right. Above and behind the lifeless figures is rock. On top of that is shrubbery surrounded by some type of greenery stretching back to tall oak trees topped with emerald, green leaves. The conglomeration is so thick you can't see the other side, except where it ends twenty-odd feet in front of me. It's the end of the beginning of the endless blue.

The screeching turns into a horrible caterwaul. From behind those trees comes a jet liner, a 747 or DC-10. Whatever it is, it's huge! It's black with a white bottom and the wing on its left side is ablaze. I give a lifeless stare, like the figures of bones, watching the flames dance across the wing.

The engine screams as it makes a sudden turn back from the endless blue. Now this gigantic crucifix of fire in the sky veers from the blue, so quickly that it has rolled on its back, flying, on the opposite side of the dried riverbed. I watch with boundless thoughts of nothing, not caring, stoic. It scrapes the top of the tall trees for a moment then disappears in the lofty timbers of this strange world.

The jet explodes and burns as flames grow high and kiss the strange sky. Hot air is forced my way caused by the impact, delirious silence fills my mind. My thoughts are woven with dissolution and disbelief of what just happened.

I stare at the smoke and flames rising from behind the wall of trees. The bones of the once tormenting people aligning the river's edge, suddenly, all at once, crumble to the ground. Piles of bones cover the walkway on both sides as dust fills the air from the sudden collapsed. The pain in my back is overwhelming; I feel slits open just inside my shoulder blades. It brings me to my knees. Looking down at the dried earth of the riverbed, blood drips from around my back and over my shoulders, starting to puddle before me. "What is happening?" I scream to the hot, blue sky, and then fall into my own pooling blood. I lay there, blood and dirt painting the side of my face. Suddenly I realize a shadow has fallen over me, blocking the hot, hot sun. Is it a man? It is hard to see through the blaring sun.

The sound of the river fills my ears once more. I turn and see a wall of turbulent water, thirty foot high, heading my way. It has come back for me, to finish my hell ride to the endless blue.

Eyes shut and expecting to be hit by a wall of water, I felt nothing except a little, cooling mist splash my body. I open my eyes to a new world, not externally but internally. A roar of water is flowing under my feet as I float just above the raging river. I look over my shoulder and see the flap of giant, bat-like wings cutting the air. I feel them strain and pull every muscle in my back. I feel strong, vibrant and irritably evil! There is a hate running through me like a raging fire. Gritting my teeth, I suddenly realize that they are not my originals. They are pointy and sharp. I prick my finger touching them. Looking at my hand, I see that I have really changed. My hands are dark-gray, thick skin dried and cracked. My nails are points of pain-giving torture. I am seeing things in a new light, or, should I say, a new dark. Everything I have done, all my dirty deeds has manifested into what I am now, and as powerful the feeling, there is a constant rage running through me that I cannot control.

Looking towards the edge of the river, I suddenly start to move there. From the flap of my wings I raise up and down in hard jerks and jumps, these things that look like bat wings are not designed for subtle flying. They are made for speed, height, distance.

Landing on the ground, pain rages through my feet up my legs, making me angry. It seems everything I do, every step I take is designed to keep me irritable, always in misery—a constant fit of rage. I walk in the middle of piled bones and that makes me angry!

A light, annoying mist starts to fall. I walk only a few more steps and could not take it anymore. Aloft I went, just above the bones that fell along the now raging river. Taking flight is a strange feeling, a feeling that I am in violation with nature.

Screw the feeling.

I fly high and furiously. I was right—these wings were made

for cutting air with speed and agility. As I loop around, I see that I leave some sort of trail, or vapor and flying back into it, the smell is horrible.

A loud explosion caught me my attention. It's coming from where the jumbo jet went down. Fire rose from behind the trees. I head over, and where the fire rises past the tree's I see little balls of whitish-silver floating up from the crash site. At first it is a couple, some in groups, just floating high into the sky. I fly closer, coming on the destruction, I hear cries of agony and insidious laughter. I hover above, and then circle the flames and fire of the wreckage. I see hundreds of bodies sprawled everywhere. And as horrific as that may be, there is something far worse. There are hundreds of creatures running around, laughing and giggling in lieu of the destruction. Like an army that just won a major battle, they run around the dead, torturing the survivors, screaming in victory.

They all look something like me...

They are me...

I circle once more, flying through unavoidable black smoke, looking over the destruction and finally swooping down on the hell below me, landing between fuselage and fire, I am barely noticed by my fellow creatures who are enjoying the spoils of a dying world. There are all types of creatures that now populate the area. Some look like me and others are small, little troll-like beings. They have hooves for feet yet I can see they are also in pain when they walk. However when they travel, they turn into little blurs that streak as they move. Others are all most human-looking from the torso up, however the other half is the body of a snake. They have fangs and any human condition is in body alone, they hiss and spit like the serpents they truly are. And truly they eat like a serpent, coming across one just in the middle of a meal. The human part of it is up, pointing to the sky with the bruised legs of a woman kicking wildly as the creature swallows her whole. She screams, but her screams are muffled as her legs disappear into this fellow demon. She is still alive. I can see her trying to kick through the beast's side. But soon after, her struggle slows, I am sure the acid is strong, eating her head as I speak. I see another two legged hag chewing on a burnt arm, there is a burning tire next to her and in the flame and burning tar I see a leg, a forearm, and other parts, maybe a rib cage, I cannot tell what they are, getting ready to be dined on. I am overwhelmed at all I see. I am standing in the middle of this hell and I know it is not only here, the world is dead, and HELL has opened up wide taking it all. Some of the creatures are trying to stop the silver-white balls from floating up, trying to catch them but to no avail, infuriating them. I move through the sporadic debris of a downed airliner. A man crawls from a wall of flames; every inch of him is on fire, his mouth a black circle, like the opening of a furnace, wide, screaming, fire is shooting from it. He lands at my feet, grabbing for my leg, I kick his hands away. A heavy odor of burnt hair fills my nose. I watch his head bubble from the fire. The old hag that was chewing an arm a moment before jumped out from nowhere onto this mans burning back. Her eyes are wide and bulging as her wings fold on her back. Open scabs are oozing puss and greenish-brown liquid, she growls at me:

"He's mine!" She said, swinging one of her deformed, clawed hands at me. As I moved away, she sunk her teeth deep into the burning flesh of the man's neck. He screamed through his mask of flames, one final cry to a mad world, and then his face fell into his own ashes. The old hag sat back in orgasmic delight, savoring the mouthful of flesh like it was a drug suddenly coursing through her veins.

With one big swoop of my wings, I take flight, straight up into

the sulfuric air of a doomed world. I stop and float on a strong
headwind from the south, looking over the strange, new landscape.
I look as far as I can see and it is nothing but true hell on earth
unfolding before me. I am a part of this now. This is what I have
become, a representation of what I truly was when I was alive. I
was a demon in sheep's clothing, and now I have transformed into
my true self.

Through the reeking evil of this world, I watch balls of silver
lifting to the sky. Up, far to the north, I see it. From the bottom of
some strange cloud, there is a string hanging from it, yes, a black
string, or what looks like a black string dropping all the way to the
ground. I let myself move with the head wind. A quarter mile is
all I needed to realize it was some sort of ladder stretching from
the ground. One of the silver balls bumped into me, I watch it drift
by and that is when I realized that all these balls are heading up to
that strange, lavender cloud formation.

An insidious scream calls my attention. I float around, a foul wind
hits my face, and what lies below me is much too horrible to tell.
Demons are on the hunt, killing and eating the flesh of human
beings. No mercy in there frenzy of gore, unleashed on the timid.
It is truly the end of the world and here I am, one of the beasts
doomed to stay here for eternity. Even for someone as evil as I, I
cannot stand to look at what is happening. I... I don't belong here.
I cannot stay here in this hell.

Again, I watch as the balls of silver float peacefully up to the
heavens. Seeing how they group together and then head to the
strange lavender clouds off in the distance.

"I know what you are." I say, to the balls as they rise to kiss
the sky. You are the souls of the good. Redemption is yours, it
was always there for the asking and I paid no mind. It was a small

price to pay and I refused. Heaven and hell will not coexist any longer. The gates of Heaven are closed to me and my kind—it's not fair! Who are they that pass judgment, who passes the laws of eternal existence! I need to know!

"Martin."

"What is brewing in that little pea-brain head of yours my dear Marty?"

I turned and there is the old hag hanging in the air, her wings flapping wildly, barely keeping her fat, grotesque body aloft, using the bone of a finger as a toothpick. She throws it over her shoulder.

"My dear, dear Martin. Why do you look to the sky, so? You shouldn't look beyond your own realm my dear Martin. You are not allowed. The Lavender City is theirs, this is ours my dear Martin." She said, looking down on a dead world with delite in her eyes.

"Mind your business, Hag"

I move in on her and with one swoop of my hand she went tumbling towards earth. I took flight, higher into the sky, I can hear her still squawking like the mad demon she is. I rose higher; her belligerent wails began to fade in the escalating hell below. Her wings could not catch her large, tumbling mass as she fell towards earth.

The sky, once you pass the noise of the chaos below is beautiful. My wings consume air, so powerful, strong, evil looking. Coming around a white cloud, I see my destination. The ladder dropping from the lavender cloud makes it easy to find. The wind of Heaven hits my face, like an invisible hand, though beautiful, it seems to be holding me back. It will do no good. I must see—I must meet my judge who cast me to damnation. I want answers and I want answers now.

Arrrrwww! A sudden pain shot through me, I am dizzy, and then again, another burst of pain, like a loud bell, with the blur of a round circle shooting out my chest. Tones of laughter erupt around me. I flapped hard and turn; four blurs of darkness were just below me.

"Martin, Martin, Martin. You know you are not allowed to go there Martin!" Four demonic voices spoke in harmony.

"Leave me be!" I yelled, then I flew, flapping my wings hard and heavy. There, where the ladder ends, that is where I must go!

I flew hard, turning to see the balls of blurs in hot pursuit. I come to the ladder and then with a sharp turn upwards I fly adjacent to reach my destination. Each rung of ladder passed me like a movie film. Something in my vision, on the ladder, I pay it no mind. Just a little more and—

They have me! Smashing my face into the metal of the ladder. I am dazed; they are small, fast, and powerful. I am pinned, I feel them zooming in and out of my body. The pain is too much, I am weakening. One hand slips off the ladder, but I hold on. One hand keeps me from falling from the sky. I am too weak, I try and flap my mighty wings but I can't. I just can't. I slip, one rung, now two and the film starts again, I—

I suddenly stop. I open my eyes and cannot believe what I see.

His arm feels soft and smooth, like a Persian rug. His whole body, in some way, reeks of kindness—it bleeds from his pores like molasses, and in some profound way, I know this, I know he is an angel from heaven, but his eyes tell me otherwise. His eyes are the only thing that tells me he was once human.

"Help meeeeeee!" I said, hideously rolling from my lips, sending a chill up my spine. I cannot believe that is my voice.

"Let him go, let him go." Sadistic whispers came from the shadows that swirl around me.

"He is evil."
"He is bad."
"He is ours!"

(rrrrrrrrrriiiipppppppppp!!!!!!!!!)

In that instant a shadow took form and ripped one of the wings from my back, the sound of a thousand newspapers being torn filled my ears, along with a horrible scream that echoed through the sky, falling long and slow upon the earth. Tears oozed from my eyes that now are rolling back into my head. I am silent, held only by the grip of his hand. A shadow took form again, this time with fangs, and sunk them deep into his arm, as he screamed to the sky, his grip broke and I began falling towards earth, followed by the shadow's giggling and laughing as we plummet like meteors, with a streak of fire tailing us.

I cannot fly. I see my wing high above me, tumbling like an autumn leaf.

I begin to tumble, faster and faster towards the hell for which I have come from. I could not help but laugh, because gazing out into the lovely sight of Demons falling to hell with me, I know now, I am truly home....

Intangible Voices

The explosion was loud, knocking me to the other side of tomorrow. The ringing in my ears echo on forever. So dark, can't see, the lights went out on that last flash, just before I went flying. I need to rest, I can't—no, I don't want to move yet. I feel mustard gas touching my face, I don't need to see or smell to know what it is. It has texture that I never noticed before, crawling over my skin. I feel fresh blood flowing through the cracks of the already dried blood on my face, I am afraid to touch my wound with dirty hands—need to rest, need to get a grip, need to breath.

The sounds around me are not comforting, through the cannon and machine gun fire, what is it? German, Japanese, Arabic? I can't tell.

I guess it doesn't really matter.

Intangible voices.

I hear screaming and trampling of the ground, I feel their boots kicking around me as they make some charge into the fog of hell from where I came. Hearing them, I freeze, perfectly still, wait—wait until it is quiet. Then it happened, I felt one of them trip over me and cuss something intangible. I hear him shuffle to his feet quickly, he is scared shitless, I can tell, camaraderie us solders share, fear does not discriminate.

Something flew from his lips, some language I do not understand. His language and ideology is irrelevant, blood still pours, it knows no language.

Dust kicked up around me, entering my already dry mouth, I turn my cheek to the cold earth and I feel his boot next to my shoulder. Something pointy is at my throat, just below my chin above the Adam's apple. It is dull, cold, and hard against my throat, it would be a messy effort for him to put it through me. Suddenly there is another pair of boots kicking dust to the right, and they were both yelling at me, boots to the side of my ribs and intangible voices giving me commands I do not understand. They went back and forth, commanding rhetoric fell on me like a heavy rain—I still don't move.

More kicks to the ribs, more bombs, more gunfire echoing this pit I fell into. Everything is turning to hell, it's hard to breath, ribs crack from steel toes, screaming, intangible voices, I can't take it anymore.

"STOP IT, GOD DAMN YOU!"

I gasp for air, my heart is in my throat, I feel the world spinning, I wish I could see, I am lost in my own darkness, gasping for air and in a choking voice I say to my assailants:

"Please help me."

Silence fell.

A cry to heaven—unanswered. A cry for salvation—ignored.

I feel the dull steel of the bayonets pressure pull away from my neck. The shoes that were kicking my ribs subsided, yet I feel them next to me still, standing, rigid, waiting.

I put my hands up to a heaven I cannot see, reaching for something beyond any god forsaken thing around me, beyond the hell of this war, beyond the madness that drifts like the yellow fog of mustard gas choking us. Like the air, fear and hate is all around me, thick and heavy, like a foul odor. I reach beyond that, I stretch outside the cloud of hate, beyond this reality of war, somewhere that—

The soldiers start to whisper. I hear the familiar sound of a match flaring to life, yet I see nothing, no light at all. I feel the heat of the match close to my face, little sparks stick to my cheek. I hear one of the men swallow hard, then words flew back and forth once more, as the match falls onto my neck.

A heavy conversation flew between them, still I do not understand.

Intangible voices.

Suddenly, the boots trampled away, loud at first, splashing mud puddles, wet earth, finally fading into the havoc of an erupting, dismal war. I froze for a moment, making sure I can't feel the presents of anything—there is nothing, I only feel the hot sting of hell—I am alone.

I turn over and crawl, the incline is steep, but I make my way up the side with loose debris slipping under foot. I must keep moving—find shelter to clean my eyes. The ground is muddy, wet, cold, but level now. Bullets are cutting the air, bombs and machine guns erupting all at once. The back and top of my head is tingling—sweating. I can't breathe through my nose, not clogged, just can't breath, as if my olfactory just dried up and shriveled away. My face is starting to hurt, must be shrapnel, I do not know.

I go on, blind, afraid to touch my wound with dirty hands; it must be a large gash because I can feel the blood pouring out of me. I feel mustard gas around my head and body, wrapping around me like an old dirty blanket. I don't need to see or smell the vapors touching me—hell's kiss—crawling slowly up my cheeks, inside my shirt—holding me, a seduction of a demon unleashed by madmen of some sardonic perversion. Nevertheless, I keep moving, I am dead if I do not find help or at least shelter soon.

A loud explosion pulls me back from my runaway thoughts. I crawl, stopping only when pattering feet go splashing by, or the sudden death-scream off somewhere floating hell's oblivion. An explosion not to far in front of me sends dust and debris into my face, I try to squint, but I can't, at least I do not have the sensation, I have no upper facial movement. I am parched, my mouth is terribly dry, the canteen at my side is near empty, but I only need a bit, just enough to spit, needing the rest to clean my now throbbing, hurting eyes.

A boot! My hand grabbing it. I hold still to see if—is he playing dead, I do not know.

No movement...

Moving my hand up, I feel the laces, nice and tight, ending in a perfect bow tie at the end. The cuff of his pants tucked into the boot with military perfection. The fabric is thick, tough, specifically made for this kind of wartime situations. I can't tell who's side he is on, is he one of ours, or one of theirs—that matters little now.

"Sorry, friend, I need your canteen."

Using his leg as a road map was a mistake, it lead right past his knee and ended at torn flesh and a jagged bone, the sinew still warm, needless to say it startled me, I should have known by the way it moved, I panicked and threw it like an old log. I got to my feet and started running, running nowhere into a war that I wanted no part of, forced here by ignorant propaganda. Everything is erupting, hearing soldiers around me, screaming incoherent garbles of madness.

Intangible voices.

Farther and farther, I feel I am going deeper, almost sinking, almost swallowed by this, this, hell. It seems as though falling, yes, that is it, falling into hell. Dante's Inferno starts to fill my mind.

'When I beheld him in the desert vast,
"Have pity on me," unto him I cried,
"Whichever thou art, or shade or real man!'

Different verses of Inferno filled my head as I ran on into my own darkness, into my own madness, until falling over what seemed like a dead cow, landing face first into broken glass, it digs into my palms and forearms. I need a minute to catch my breath. Something solid is in front of me, don't ask me how I know. I feel it looming over me like a tower. Crawling slowly, reaching out, for what, I do not know, maybe for salvation, maybe for the hand of God. However, that is not what I found, I found structure. Sure enough, the edge of a building is before me. I slide down its side feeling my way along the brick facade, looking for an entrance, it cannot be far, it must—here, the entrance to this building.

A draft of cool air hits me, like standing at the entrance of a deep cave. The door is non-existent; I fall in, dropping about a half a foot onto compacted dirt.

"Hello?" I said. "I need help!"

No response.

The interior of this place feels empty and cold. Hollow of the love that was once here before the war frightened it away. The thick walls that once protected family secrets muffle the hell outside. The only sound is a drip echoing somewhere in my darkness, grabbing my attention fully, calling me to clean my eyes of the blood and debris that fills them.

Moving quickly at first, I bumped into something, I need to take my time and listen to my surroundings, focusing on the drip until it is the only thing I can hear. Nothing else mattered except that annoying sound off in the distance. I walked around tables and chairs, surprised that they are in one piece, considering how bad this area has been shelled. I walked until I hit a wall, following it to a door. I feel the bullet holes that riddled the wood like Swiss cheese, it fell open from the slightest push, old and tired, just giving up. I feel that just from opening the door.

Standing in the doorway, suddenly a shadow darts before my path. A little joy comes over me, with a slight touch of fear, I must be getting my sight back. I can't make out what it is however, it is there, moving slowly at first, and then darting in the corner of the room.

Is it a child?

For some reason I do not feel threatened, if it is going to kill me then so be it. However, my eyes are burning, I need water now.

In the far end of the room, the drip calls me. I hear it echoing the walls, sounding pure, sweet, like the voice of a beautiful, sexy woman, and my dry throat begs for its soothing moisture. I reach out, sure enough the cold metal is there, smooth and inviting. Standing over it, the drips of water echo in my ears. I turn behind me, the shadows presence is there, not moving, just subtle movements from agitation. How I can see nothing else but the shadow of human existence is frightening, it starts to mumble something I cannot make out.

Intangible voices.

I reach for the nozzle, it's cold, wet steel sent a chill through my whole body, I move my hand over it, feeling the leaks where the valves and connectors are. The handle is raised and curved, finding its end I give it a gentle heave downward. Water flowed like a waterfall, sounding serene and soothing. I touch the flowing stream, it is luke warm at first, then cold, refreshing water flows over my hand. The excitement is overwhelming. I give it a few good, hard pumps and put both hands under the soft water. I try to wash the heavy dirt off and then pooling the water in my hands, dowsing my face with the clean—

"AAAAAAHHHHH!!!!!!!!!!!!!!"

Am I awake? I am not sure, the world is still black. Could I be dreaming? No. I would see my dream, and the pain, my God; the pain feels like my face is sitting in a frying pan of sizzling bacon fat. The rest of my body is burning of a different feeling, some sort of fever now. I try to lift my head, but I can't. Am I dying?

What happened, I just—

Laying in my darkness, a deep fear rose to the top of my throat. I lift my hand in front of my face, not thinking I would see it, but in hesitation of what I am about to do. I close and open it, feeling the sensation of its movement, every tendon and nerve. I feel the tightness behind and just below the knuckles, and how the pressure frees on their extension. Yes, it is working perfectly, working perfectly to feel the mangled outline of my face. I hear someone crying, is it me? No. I am too stoic and too sick to cry. It is not a cry of fear or hurt, but a cry of loss, maybe even loneliness. Yes, as soft as it is, it is the cry of a child—a girl. I am curious, but for now, I pay no attention, I let it slip from my mind. I am in serious trouble.

Gently I touch the outline brow of my eye, which is where I think I start anyway. Like a man lost without a map—nothing here seems right. The terrain is deformed and unfamiliar. I feel hot blood run slowly down the crown of my face. What else could it be? I have no eyes to shed tears, they are gone, lost in the propaganda of someone else's war. My nose is the dust of ignorance. On the edge of my wound, I feel the crisp, burned flesh, moving inward, I feel the soft sinew of my wound. There is a sunken cavity where my nose once was. The outline of my eye sockets are also deep pools of darkness. Reality of this horror sent my mind in a spin of delirium. I am in a world of blackness the rest of my life, how will I get out of here? What will I do? I have no one. These things run through my mind, I can't catch my breath. The pain in my skull has intensified from my new realization. It feels like my brain is slowly leaking from my skull—I can't stay awake—I—

At first, my vision is blurred, but yes, I can see. The image of a flower forms in my eyes. I don't know what kind it is, however it is orange, intricate and beautiful, dipping from a soft wind. I am lying in a grassy field laced with soft dew. Looking up into a blue sky, I sit up suddenly, just able to look over the field of grass that rolls down hill from where I am. I touch my face where the tear streams down, it is familiar, my face is normal.

I stumble to my feet, the open field seems to roll forever throughout the valley. A sound caught me, I turn and see a child, up the hill, Laughing, calling to me.

"Come on, we have to go!"

I look around, expecting to see someone behind me, nothing there, just dancing grass all around. I turn to look at her.

"Come on, will you!"

She turned and disappeared over the rim of the hill. I look on in puzzlement, but I could not resist. I started up the hill. However, something else now is calling me. I turn to a rumbling thunder. Black clouds swirled behind me. They came fast from nowhere, I see heavy rain off in the distance. I start to run, something tells me to get over the hill, you will be safe, I run, a sudden flash of lightning, it hit me right in the head, things go black for a moment, then blurry, then I focus. I stumble, but I keep moving. Another bolt of lightning right into my head, inverted colors filled my vision, the top is too far, I will not make it, another flash and my world is black.

The sensation of waking is strange. When you go from sleep to wake with no eyes, it is no different from walking into another room. No eyes to open or close to distinguish from wake and sleep, it is just another reality, and walking into a wall of sheer pain.

The pain is so intense, what is even worse I can't even squint my eyes to cringe from it.

However, distraction helps.

Someone is rummaging through the pockets of my uniform. I do not move at first, I wait, first through thigh pockets, moving up to the hip. I hear him breathing. Heavy—out of breath. His hands shake like a desperate alcoholic. I feel him moving up to my shirt. As he pulled the Craven-A cigarettes from my pocket my hand snaps out and grabs his. He screamed like a scared child.

"Good God, good God!" He broke my grip and slid back against the wall.

"You, you are alive!"

I said nothing. I just listen for his next move, waiting for that shot into my skull to end my misery. However, all I can hear is his breathing, nothing else. I flinch from the sudden sound of a match flaring to life, and then the exhale from a long drag.

I feel him looking at me, trying to figure me out, why I am not dead. I try to hold back the pain, but he must notice the agony of my quivering lips.

"You Americans have the best smokes." He waits for a response, I give none. I hear him shuffle and stir, probably from anticipation of what I will do—I play dead, no movement, he has the advantage but I will not play his game. Exhaling long and hard, he said: "Do you want me to kill you?"

I sit up and turn looking into his direction, and what a sight I must have been, staring without a face, is he looking at me? Can he look at me? My tough guy exuberance only lasts for a moment and I had to lie back, I am starting to get incredibly weak and he knows it.

"I should kill you, however from the looks of things, you are already dead my friend."

Reaching for my holster, I hear him move, then nothing.

"Don't waste your time, your holster is empty."

Sure enough, he was right. My sidearm is long gone. The long whistle of an incoming, I hear him run for cover, an explosion shook the building like an earthquake. The dust falling from the rafters found my wound and the pain is searing, feeling like fire scorching my face.

I begin to scream.

He tries to quiet me.

"Shut up you bastard, they will find us!" I did not listen, I screamed—drowning out his heavily accented commands until I felt the butt of a rifle hit the side of my skull. I felt lost for a moment, the pain vibrated through my wound like electricity. I can hear him cussing to himself, then another blow, the pain went away and I can see again.

Wet grass again surrounds me. I fluttered my eyes to beams of sunlight breaking through escaping black clouds off in the corner of the sky. I sat up on top of the hill, looking down into the valley. It is wet and wonderful. Remembering the little girl, I turn and look up towards the hill. Standing is difficult, but I manage and head up to the top of the hill.

The hill is steeper than anticipated. I turn once more to see if there is another storm heading my way, all I see is the sun and bits of black clouds sinking behind another mountain range as though being flushed. At first, there is no sound, like watching a silent movie. However, slowly it comes in, and the sound of this place is as wonderful as it looks.

Breaking its crest, the valley sinks into itself, melting with beautiful blues and greens, covered in the dew of the recently fallen rain. Moreover, in those blue and greens lies the outline of a village blending in the center of this beautiful collage of weaving reality. The air is crisp, with a sting of fall in it, tree's sway in the outskirts of town. Everything is moving slowly here, a pace undefined by normal reality and the reality of my mind. The wind that blows off the hills is like a soothing hit of opium, harsh at first, then smooth like a touch of velvet.

A child's laughter rides the sullen winds, pulling my attention to no one place in particular but suddenly she seemed to just appear. Yes, it is that strange. And there she is, walking towards me in knee-high grass. She is little, dirty, and her hair a hornet nest of tangles. However, her smile shined through the dirt like the sun gleaming off chrome. Suddenly she is next to me, a little higher than my knee, looking up as though looking up at the curiosities of the sky. She grabbed my index finger, pulling me towards the village below. At its edge, were a line of people there waiting for us, waving and calling, but the voices, I could not understand.

Intangible voices.

However, there is an understanding, and I feel welcome. And just because I cannot understand their words, I feel warmth that is overwhelming and accepting. It is strange, but it is here that I feel I belong.

Suddenly thunder roared in the distant. My little friend stopped and looking into the corner of the sky and then back at me. I knew what it was, and so did she.

I am used to it now.

Shit!

Finally, I turn looking at her, I said: "Don't you worry, next time I will stay much longer, I will find a way."

Through teary eyes, she just smiled.

The thunder is a steady flow of noise. I again woke to darkness. What was thunder now turned into a siren wailing. Voices over me were soothing yet loud. "You will be ok, we found you just in time. Good thing we heard you screaming, we would never have found you in that house."

I passed out.

I have been doing that a lot lately.

* * *

"What happened to me on that battlefield changed me forever."

"Go on." I am sure he is paying no attention to me, probably scribbling little boxes and squares, lost in his own problems swirling his mind.

I say nothing.

Somewhere water drips with an annoying echo, ever since my experience in the house, dripping water drives me crazy. After a moment the scribbling stops. I feel his stare through the darkness.

"Please, go on."

"How about just letting me sleep... Forever." I said half joking.

"Why do you want to die?"

"I didn't say die, I don't want to die, are you listening? I want to sleep—as I said—forever."

After a moment, a stale, stoic voice said: "You were just in a coma for a day and a half, don't you think that was long enough?"

His voice echoes the chambers of my ears, bouncing into the darkness.

I waited a moment and said: "That is when I truly live."

Silence.

"I can't have them put you to sleep just because you are depressed, and even if I—"

Intangible voices.

He continues to talk. However, I don't listen. It is useless to try to make him understand. My thoughts fade to the permanent darkness that I experience day in and day out as long as I am awake in this world. This man-made darkness has a way to pull you into it, absorbing you like a sponge. It is synthetic, created by minds of greed, anxiety and cowardice's—a manifestation, a representation of who they are, and I am continuously reminded of them by continuously looking into the void they so generously gave me. And sometimes if I concentrate hard, sometimes I can even see them moving in the darkness of my minds-eye. Trying to hide, but I catch them, slithering and hiding, yet, there is nothing I can do to stop them. Money rules the world, and because of that, people continue to die.

What a surprise.

For the remanding years at the hospital, I did what they wanted. I listened to them, took their pills, drank their drinks, and waited. Finally, in the name of rehabilitation, they let me leave the hospital.

I was let go.

The knock at the door was loud. I sit up in bed, sweating heavily all over my body. Most people fall asleep to darkness, I wake to it and the frustration that never seems to go away. Again the knock, I feel for my scarf on the end table to cover my faceless features. I don't want to scare off my dealer.

That's a joke.

My room is a twenty-by-twenty shit-hole. All the comforts of home are here in one place. There are no walls dividing anything, it is all in the open. The shitter is in the corner, right next to the bed. At the opposite end, there is a small stove, and that is it.

The knock came again, much louder this time.

I touch the door.

"Is that you?" I say, just above a whisper.

"Yeah, open up, I ain't got all day!" I undo the four locks and slide the chain off its latch. I do not have to ever see Niko to know what he looks like. His voice describes him for me, and even though I have not been able to smell things, my taste buds have taken over. I can taste his bad cologne drifting the air before he even walks in.

"Good God!" He said. "What is that smell!" He moaned.

I said I am used to it.

That is a joke.

He came in, the kitchen table is next to the door—I sit down. He falls in the chair opposite me. I reach out for my smokes, Niko already helped himself, I hear the flare of a lighter, I hear the exhale of smoke and he reaches for my hand, giving me the cigarette.

How kind of him.

"How can you live like this, man?"

With my olfactory gone, I have to take short, little puffs and exhale quickly, or I get the sensation of not breathing. It was scary at first, but you get used to it.

He takes a long drag, and with what seems an even longer exhale says: "Man, that smell is bad, man!"

"Nice to chat with you too, Niko."

A long sigh and he says: "Why is it, that all you do is sleep, man?"

Right to the point, I always like that about him.

I feel his exhale of smoke wrap around my forehead; I taste the smoke lingering in front of me, making its way into my mouth, and that smoke, tells me everything about this thug sitting across from me. Woven in it is tiny bits of saliva, he has rotten teeth, I taste metal—Heroin. Heroin swims in this man's veins, thick, slow, flowing like a sewer. He is high now. I taste starch, quinine swimming his breath. He shoots pure shit, there is a slight taste of Naloxone, I know it from the hospital—he recently OD'd.

What a shocker.

That's no joke.

If I had eyes, the look of disgust would have killed him. However, I cannot intimidate this loser—I need him.

A siren outside breaks the simmering silence.

"Do you have the stuff?" I say, not answering his other questions. Ignoring Niko is not the smartest thing to do, even for a thug, he will not hit a deformed cripple, just take full advantage whenever possible. He already gets most of my money through buying his drugs, I eat very little, and when I sleep for days, I wake famished, but a few crackers and a little stale bread creates nausea, killing hunger quickly.

Another long exhale, I hear the bag hit the table. I reach out feeling my way, finding them I suddenly feel his calloused hand grab mine, for a drug dealer, his hand is like sand paper. "Where is the money my friend, no dollar bills this time."

He Laughs.

I am wearing my army jacket, the very one that I had on the day my government took my eyes, nose and sinuses. The weeks that followed, I would sleep with it crunched up like a pillow. Many times, they tried to take it from me, they said it is saturated with dried blood, still, I would not let them. Whatever I do, wherever I go, it is on me—always.

I reach into the pocket that says, US Army, feeling its perforation like Braille, pulling out thirty ten-dollar bills. I hear him snicker. I count to verify, I reach out for the pills until I find them, I hand the money to him. He can't stop snickering.

What a dirt bag.

I hear him get up from the chair, his footsteps fall heavy heading to the door.

"You know, if you ever need a woman—" He stops in mid stride, "or whatever turns you on, I could have them here in ten minutes, providing you got the money—which I know you got. And let me tell you, man, they won't care about—what you are."

"And what am I?"

I couldn't resist.

" You know, dirty, filthy—a freak." I can hear the grin crack across his face.

He is trying to intimidate me. The anger builds, but I just say: "No thank you."

He is silent, telling me he is looking around my room, perhaps looking for a stash.

After a moment, I hear the doorknob turn. I feel the draft from the outside world touch me with an unforgiving slap, reminding me how clean it is, even though the doorway only opens to a dirty hallway.

Outside my door, his voice is loud and echoing. "I will be in touch my friend."

I say nothing.

Shutting the door, I bolt and latch all my locks, closing the door to a reality that I do not want any part of anymore. This world has taken too much from me, it is unforgiving and ruthless, and the people that run it are hostile and evil. The wars for profit seem to go on forever in the name of democracy.

Therefore, through sleep, I run away, because there, in my dreams, I can see. I see places that greed cannot go. Don't get me wrong, I do not want to die, I am afraid of death, which is where this place and the people in it tried to send me. They removed my eyes, but I still see, I see right through them. Even though the candle of my soul is dim, I do not want it to go out in the fluttering harsh winds of reality.

After downing six sleeping pills, I sit at the edge of my bed. They go down hard, my throat trying to reject them, and after a moment, my stomach has something to say violently. Six is enough to let me sleep but not enough to kill me. I do not think so anyway, it is hard to say if you cannot see. Before I lay my head on a pillowcase that I have not washed in years, I hear the sudden laughter of children outside my window. It startles me at first, having not heard anything outside these windows except loud cars honking and the occasional swearing for years. Fights above me happen nightly, I am surprised she is not dead yet, but surely, like me, she is dead inside.

However, those kids playing outside lit something inside me. For the first time, I feel a little calm. A sudden serenity came over me. Yes, it could be the pills, but I do not think so. I hear them playing war, the fake sounds of gunfire echo through my room and somehow, it is soothing. The innocence of future warmongers, it makes me laugh.

I lay back, feeling the dirty pillow wrap my head. The bed itself would make me feel like bugs were crawling over me, and when you can't see, that is as good as real. However, not this time. It feels like the inside silk of a coffin, so relaxing, so wonderful. I feel the onslaught of sleep, crawling from my feet upward, the darkness starts to pulse, swirl and liquefy into vibrant colors. I see the shadows that hid in my darkness run lost through the streams of bright hues. They can't hide so they turn and yell something intangible.

Intangible voices.

I simply ignore them, walking away. Stepping into the grassy field, up to the top of the hill, and just over it, my home, the place where I can see.

Renina the Ice Dancer

A black, rotary phone echoes from the hallway. Running the walls to the kitchen in the back of the house where a mother sits stoic, stirring her morning tea. Jumping to the sound, her hair stands frigid running to the phone. Making a sharp right in the living room, she runs past the old cellar door, running the hallway of the stairs and catches the phone on its third ring.

"Hello, Hello?" She said with quick, nervous tones.

"Oh, hello mom." said with a bit of frustrated relief.

"Fine, fine. And you?"

"No the doctor hasn't called yet"

"Yes I know, if he doesn't get a donor soon there could be problems"

"Yes I know, more than problems"

"But I trust Dr. Gilda, he will find a donor"

"Oh, he's fine, been very weak though, and a bit pale but he's holding up fine"

"Yes mom I will tell him, I love you too"

"Good bye." Saying those words she gives a long, worried look up the staircase to the second floor.

* * *

Curtains float rakishly out a second floor window, while the shine of a chilly morning dances on the interior walls. The shimmering diamonds create an array of shapes and images of nature's secret code, unbreakable by the ignorance of the human mind.

An ashen boy stands with arms stretched, inhaling the beautiful morning, breathing deep, and exhaling the invigorating air into the chilly room while goose bumps grow all over his young, pale body.

Eye's shut he absorbs the beautiful late, winter morning. He is lost in another place, another time, lost in the world of a young boy's mind, a place where you and I are not allowed to go. Yes it is chilly—oh, how his body tells him so, but he is warm, warm in his own solitude—warm in his home and that makes Joshua Weaver smile.

He has been away for three weeks, home two days and gone three weeks more. The hospital was his temporary home, and a painful one at that! However that's all forgotten now, he is finally home, in his room and that's all that matters, just the smell of a boy's room and the God given freedom to open the windows in winter.

"ARE YOU CRAZY!" Followed with a sudden jerk on his arm and back to reality.

"DON'T YOU REALIZE IF YOU CATCH COLD YOU COULD DIE!" Her eye's bulging out of her head.

"But mom I—Well I, I was—the hospital was so stuffy and hot and—I am just so happy to be home"

Her eyes welled with tears, and she grabbed her son, and that instant the closet door flew wide open and a little pirate shot out with sword wielding—cutting the air!

"Ahoy there swashbuckler!" Then with the sweet, tone of a little boy:

"Hey, it's cold in here"

The laughter erupts, bouncing the walls, grabbing her boys she squeezes hard, she is happy to have everyone under one roof again.

It's been a long day in the Weaver house. The sun is setting and a white-cold fills the air in Towaco. Shutting the door with his foot, Josh brings in the night's logs off the back porch for the fire. The logs are frost covered but seasoned and will burn nicely throughout the night. The cold dew on the windows tells him that it will be a cold one and he better get a few more to let thaw by the fire.

Outside the air is crisp and clean. Josh looks at the bare, gigantic oak tree towering over him like a haunting phantom, dividing the two houses on the old farm. He notices the many leaves that were not picked up in the fall, which must come up soon before the ass of a landlord bitches at his mother for not following her lease obligation. Yes, this was the farm of his great grandfather, in the family for generations. But over the years, the farm stopped supporting itself. It used to sell to the local markets and grocery stores but that became too difficult. They wanted better quality and much cheaper prices. The stubborn old goat that Edison Jacobus was, he refused. So the sales dried up, and so did the land. Soon after, his grandfather started losing his mind. Chased all the relatives away, no one had seen him in years, and when he died, he owed so much in back taxes that the land was sold at auction. His granddaughter, Josh's mother, moved her family back under the rules of a new landlord. Sure, she could have lived anywhere but she chose this place. This is where she grew up, and she just wanted to come home for a little while, to feel the security she once had. But it's not the same. The farm, the land, it all died with her grandfather. This is not the Jacobus Farm anymore. What used to be alive and beautiful is dead, just a decaying place lost in Jersey.

While gathering logs, a strange feeling suddenly came over him, a feeling so weird that he dropped what he had, a feeling that he is being watched. The feeling begins to burn the nape of his neck, with sudden fear engulfing him. He turns to try and pin-point the feeling through the gray evening of his surroundings, suddenly re-alizing its coming from the house next door. The house is smaller than the main house that he lives in, built in the early twenties for the help that his grandfather employed to work on the farm. Josh heard the many stories that went on in the old house, but the one that scared him most was that of the murder. Ever since Josh was very small, the house seemed stuck in time, not part of the world that he and everyone else lived in. However, his fears eased when his aunt moved in with her two daughters. But the safe feeling did not last long because strange things began happening, his aunt was always oblivious to everything, lost in her own little world. But the children seemed frightened by something that cannot be seen, or something only they could see, an entity or something that Josh could not explain for the life of him.

His cousin Lilac is staring with an evil grin out the second story window. Lilac, a relative from his father's side of the family is one of twins. He knows it's her because she has pure white hair, which he can clearly see through the dirty screen that is distorting her face, looking the true evil that she is, and where there is one the other is near by. Sure enough, there was Lily, identical to Lilac except for the jet-black hair running the length of her back, standing down at the edge of the garden, in the long dead rhubarb patch. The dead rhubarb patch is a creepy place all together. It reminds Josh of dead octopuses—a garden of dead octopuses.

In unison, in his head, he heard their voices: "Welcome home Josh!" Without the slightest movement of their lips, just grins stretching across their faces sent chills through his sickly body.

He is overcome with fear even more than before, knowing now the cause! He swallows cold air, it is thick like water, hard going down. Quickly he grabs a few more logs, then heads inside. Not taking his eyes off his cousins, he stumbles and falls in the kitchen doorway, dropping his cargo. Slamming the door with his feet, he stumbles to his knees looking through one of four panels of the kitchen door. It took him only a few seconds to get to the window and already his cousins were gone, nowhere to be seen. Relieved to be inside he heads to the living room and falls in his grandfathers old chair, wheezing.

As he rests, he can't help remembering about that hot day in August, three years ago. "Poor Mr. Smith" he said out loud, sweating a bit from his nervousness, he sinks deep in his grandfather's old, chair. He literally forgot about the twins while in and out of the hospital the last few months, but seeing Lily and Lilac just now brought that horrible day flooding back to him.

It was extremely hot that August. Heat waves dance on the road and the sweat poured out of Walter Smith while he mowed his lawn with his new rider mower. The grass is low and some spots brown, but he cuts the short stubs anyway because he loves the straight lines his new mover leaves in the sun scorched grass. Plus the fact he is bored, and needs to keep himself occupied after his retirement from the pharmacy that he owned for more than thirty-five years.

The girls were playing in the sand box behind the house, lost in their thoughts and playing little girl games.

The tree house Josh acquired was on the other side of the garden nestled in the tree line lost in the foliage of greens and browns. It was old and the wood withered, a true chameleon lost in the shadow of the woods. The Nickels boys abandoned it long ago for something unimaginable to Josh—girls, but nonetheless he was more than happy to take over proprietorship of the coolest tree house in all of Towaco.

The walls reek of boy-hood dreams and fantasies of long ago. The old, grey, cobwebs dangled the corners with dead spiders swinging in its center. Like a pendulum pushed by an occasional wind, holding many secrets of dreams lost from imaginations that drifted upwards, clinging to the dusty, grey silk.

He can see everything from this position. The silhouette of the old barns off in the distance stand dark in the August haze, the two houses, even the overgrown runway of the Towaco Airport that stretches deep into the woods is visible from here. It gave him a view of the whole farm, anyone coming from the house will be spotted before the screen door slammed his or her ass.

However, August will be the end of a serenity that once flowed through the town of Towaco. On this day, something evil came, or, something dark woke from a long nightmarish sleep that lay dormant in the unseen shadows of Towaco. Josh was soaking in the heat of his little escape—almost sleeping from the heaviness of the thick humidity he lies in. It was a lazy afternoon no different from any other humid day in his town, but today is somehow strange. Earlier, Josh went uptown this morning to get his monthly comic book fix, something he did every first Saturday of the month like clockwork. The new Fantastic Four, number one hundred and twenty was due and he couldn't miss it. But the walk in the hot day was wasted. The new books didn't come and he was kicked hard with disappointment. However, when Josh walked out of the store something struck him as odd. A feeling grabbed him right behind the ears and squeezed. There was something more going on in the center of town, something strange—it was way too quiet. The people were distant; they had a look like they forgot something and it was torturing them trying to remember. People were lost, so they seemed, disorientated with where they were. They were not the friendly people that Josh knew growing up most of his life, yes, there was something definitely wrong all right. Maybe because it was too damn hot, Josh didn't know, but really he didn't care. No new comic books usually lit the dark side of Josh. Besides the oddness of everything, he brushed it off, paying no mind, however the strangeness around him would not go away and it bloomed into a flowering nightmare in the hot, August afternoon.

Josh woke from his hazy daze. Looking around, he realized it is awfully dark for this time of day in the late afternoon. He heard the tree house moan from the shifting trees blowing in a strange, hard wind. He felt the wind lean hard on one side and then the other, rocking back and forth like a freighter going across one of the great lakes in a raging storm. He looked out into the humid day, into black clouds boiling up, over the houses and the barns. What is going on, Josh thought, and then suddenly, over the violent winds, he heard one of his cousins screaming. He couldn't tell which one it was, but he can see her and she is hanging on the edge of the sand box with her feet flapping in the strong wind. However she could not keep her grip from the chaos erupting around her, this wind was so powerful that she looked like clothes on a clothesline on a windy day. She let go and she was gone—flying off around the corner of the house, taken by some force that Josh could not fathom.

Even though Josh couldn't see what was happening, he heard

their cries. He hurried to the exit and down the rickety boards haphazardly nailed into the side of the tree, breaking one of the steps, falling to the moss-covered trunk. He sat there for a moment trying to gather his thoughts, then got up and ran around the edge of the garden. He cut through the old rhubarb patch and came up on the sandbox where they were playing. Barbie dolls and clones of Barbie dolls were sporadic throughout the sandbox, waiting for the next adventure of a young girls mind. Josh felt the invisible force; it was not pulling him, but rather pushing him, and definitely not strong enough to hold him back. Whatever it was, it did not want him.

Josh was able to get to the corner of the house. He tries hard to peer around the corner, it feels like an invisible hand pushing on his head, but he manages to see around the house. He see's his cousin, its Lily being dragged across the stone driveway heading towards the opening of the well. Like an old newspaper blowing in the wind, she's bouncing and tumbling across its hard surface. Her sister is nowhere to be seen, but somehow, Josh knows her fate, her screams were different, they are echoing long and forever through the tube of the well—she is already down its hungry mouth. In a blink from the tormenting wind, he could see Lilly's head sticking out the top of the well. Her eyes and mouth were wide with agony as she tried to hold anything that would prevent her from falling into its opening. Her head is twisting and distorting, morphing to something evil, finally sinking into the hole of the well—she was gone! The screams were horrific, bouncing off the sides of the house and barns that surround the area. They seemed to come from everywhere, even the drain gutters that lay along Jacksonville road were echoing with a child's terror.

The cries began too fade along with the wind that prevented him from moving. He ran to the edge of the well and looked at the broken planks that once halfheartedly covered the dark hole in the earth. There was a stench coming from it that almost made him vomit, the screams of his cousins subsided but the well was moaning, like it was alive. Josh was lost, looking down the round hell that his relatives drank from for generations, lost in something not of this world anymore.

"What the hell is going on, Josh?"

Josh turned to see Walter Smith. The stout, bald man was panting and hot, lost in confusion of what he had seen through the heat waves from across the street.

"My cousins, they—"

"Good God, boy, they fell down the well? I told Bernard to cement this damn thing up years ago, but that bastard refused! Too costly he said, too damn costly!"

"Come on, Josh help me with that ladder!"

Josh looked at the side of the old barn where Walter was pointing. There hung on old nails was the extension ladder that has not been moved in years. Cobwebs were thick in between its rungs and who knew that aluminum could rust.

It was just long enough to touch the bottom. After the rattle and clanking of adjusting the ladder into the hole, Walter Smith stared at Josh in confusion from the horrible, deep moans that came from the well. No little girls were making that noise however he knew they were down there, he seen them fall in with his own eyes.

"I'll need a flashlight, a big one!"

Josh nodded and turned, heading for the house. He knew exactly where to go. Being in a big, creepy old house, he knows where the flashlights are. He flew like a gazelle, he was amazed how easily he glided over the lawn and into the back door of his house. He went straight to the junk drawer and there it was, sitting right on top. No sooner had the back door slammed; Josh was back at the mouth of the well giving the light to Walter.

"You wait here." He said, setting his foot on the rung of the latter.

Josh watched the old pharmacists head disappear into the darkness as he descended downwards. He heard the clanking and felt the vibrations of his steps as he held the ladder steady. He watched the flashlight float the dark, round walls of the well. He listen to Walter call his cousins by name, but only heard the echoes of his own voice.

"Do you see anything yet? Josh said, looking down the black hole of the well.

"No, not yet, I 'm only halfway down.

Walter shined his flashlight to the bottom—nothing. Waves of disturbed dust float through the rays of light like a curtain of misty rain. He shook his head, wiping the sweat from his brow. There is nothing at the bottom of this fucking well except dirt and cobwebs. He looked at the dingy round walls surrounding him. They were solid cement, a fine job indeed, built by old man Jacobus himself. Its diameter is slightly bigger than the norm, roughly six feet wide and drops two hundred feet into the earth, with smaller pipe holes burrowing in certain spots of its sides that most likely lead to the garden. Walter shined his light down one of the holes but could only see about six feet where the pipe bent. He looked down, then up, then started descending further into the darkness. The clack of his footsteps echoed the round walls, hurting his ears. The sound of the wind had a steady flow running through the well making it sound like a pipe organ playing a haunting tune, very strange for something that is supposed to end two hundred feet down. He stopped about eight feet from the bottom. A protruding pipe about five inches wide caught his attention. The hole was black, and dirt was falling from the entrance. Just as he pulled the flashlight over it, a ball of fur flew out of the hole. Walter screamed and a rat the size of a cat fell from the opening. His feet slipped from the rungs and he fell to the bottom of the well, hitting hard, landing on his left shoulder, a loud crack was heard, and he yelled long and hard. "Mr. K, you alright?" Walter heard fall from above.

His feet were tangled in the ladder. He tried getting up, but it is hard with a fucking rat attacking you. Walter did his best to fight off the little bastard. He felt little sharp pins in his arm, in his cheek, even his bald head. Again more attacks to his arms, hands and neck, he could do nothing but cover, he needed a minute to think, but there is no slowing of this rat trying to eat him. Finally he is able to kick his feet free from the ladder and maneuver his body around, find his flashlight and in one motion land a good blow to the disgusting ball of fur. It was dazed, Walter wasted no time; again and again he came down with the light, it looked like lightning flashing every time he came down on the soon to be dead bastard. It stopped moving. It lay in blood that's pooling around it. One final blow, hitting it so hard the light slipped from his hand.

Walter lay at the bottom of the well. His shoulder and chest were killing him. He's having a hard time catching his breath. The flashlight is just behind the ladder with a flag of dust waving in its beam.

"Mr. K!" Again, fell from above.

Where in the hell are those damn kids? He thought, looking up at the little round hole of sky above him and saw a head of Josh peering down.

"Are you OK?" Said the boy.

"Yes—No!" Was the reply.

His bald head felt the dirt and sediment that accumulated over the years when this well was full of water. A strange odor hit him from the side and that's what called his attention to the four foot plus black hole that was next to him. He sat up quickly sitting opposite the cave opening. He couldn't believe his eyes. This hole was not made when this well was dug. The edges are jagged and ripped, as if it were made with some ones bare hands. Walter tried to move, using the ladder to help himself up without taking his eyes off the cave entrance. A sudden wind of stench flowed, making his eyes water profusely. It was so bad he could barely look into the cave. A moment had past and finally, he was able to look deep into the opening. Water dripped into puddles and something darted in the shadows deep in the far distance. Walter is frozen, shining the light from one side to the other, looking for any slight reason not to enter the cave.

An eerie sound came from the hole, which is almost good enough reason for him not to go.

"Lily, is that you, honey?" He heard nothing but obscure noises from a strange, unnatural wind.

"Shit!" He knows what he has to do. He has to go in.

He swallowed hard, ducking down, entering the cave halfheartedly.

"Shit, shit, shit!"

Instantly his back started to hurt, he goes to straighten up but is suddenly stopped by the low ceiling hanging over him. He felt the loose debris fall on his head and neck, giving him the willies as he quickly tries to wipe it away. It is cold down here, cold as hell. Walter wiped the sweat from his head, but it came back as fast as he could wipe it away.

The cave is dingy and wet and smelled of dead animals. Bones are strewn throughout the bottom of its floor. Strange moans were coming again from the opposite end and Walter does not like it at all. Something not natural is here. He can sense it, something inside tells him to run, but something else is gripping his curiosity of the unknown. His flashlight scours the walls and follows it to the opening at the opposite end. He can see where this strange hole ends, and just as he lifted the light, a hulking, dark figure ran across the entrance. Walter froze, water dripped on his head, he did not move.

"Girls?" He said, hoping maybe—

A jolt of pain hit him in the chest, the flashlight shook and shuttered from the strain as it spread to his arm, intensifying his fear and anxiety. His breathing is becoming difficult. He leans against the tunnel wall, feeling the hand of God squeezing his heart. He hung his head, watching his sweat drip into a stagnant puddle at his feet. A moment passed when suddenly a horrific odor filled his nose once more. He tried to shake it but couldn't. As he struggles with his pain, something deep inside his body told him to look up, but fear, or maybe denial or even his slow coming heart-attack is playing a hideous game with his mind. Nonetheless he looks.

This is something he will regret doing for the rest of his life.

At the end of the tunnel stood a dark hulking mass, slowly swaying in a strange, coiling fog. It's breathing hard, sounding like its inhaling the smoke of burning rubber—hard and heavy, like it was about to keel over and die from emphysema. Beams of light broke and shot out from behind this thing as it rocked slowly side to side. Walter's eyes were tearing badly and wide with fear. His heart was hurting, beating hard in his throat. He put his hand on his chest and through his soaking wet shirt can feel the cold, clamminess of his skin. He started to back up slowly, swallowing hard, his breathing now erratic. He stumbles, stepping in a puddle, it is cold and murky, one foot soaking wet. He cussed, however not taking his eyes off the thing. Just as Walter is about to exit the hole, the thing at the other end screamed a blood curdling scream, starting a charge towards Walter. Walter was out of the hole and already

climbing the ladder. He climbed fast, even though his left arm
is giving him trouble. His hands are clammy and cold. Strange
sounds and heavy breathing echo all around him as he climbs, and
the higher he goes the louder it gets, this thing is getting closer. He
hurries, good God does he hurry. Coming up to the edge, he sees
Josh looking over the rim. Suddenly, screams of horror were coming from the well. Walter felt the thing grab the ladder below. He
felt it through the cold aluminum, and this is when all hell broke
loose!

Walter started to scream in terror. The ladder that Josh was
holding began to violently thrash back and forth—he couldn't keep
his hands on it. The moans grew louder almost drowning Walter
Smiths cries. The light from the flashlight was gone and the ladder
slowed its violent thrash. Josh heard the sudden clanking of feet
on rungs once more. Walter or something was coming out of the
hole. Josh heard whimpers and heavy breathing—he hoped it was
Walter, taking a chance he grabbed the ladder once more holding it
firm. A blood dripping bald head came out of the darkness of the
well. He looked up, eyes wide, and the blood beaded down to the
back of his scalp.
The ladder began to thrash once more. Walter could barely keep
himself from falling back into the well. He could not hold on any
longer, he let go, grabbing the edge. The ladder violently thrashed,
hitting Walter several times in the back as he clung to the side, then
suddenly it crumbled down into the mouth of the well, as though
it was eating it. Walter hung there on the edge, loosing his grip.
Josh grabbed him, pulling with all his strength, and finally, pulling
Walter Smith from the mouth of his almost demise.

Walter staggered to his feet then over to the oak tree and collapsed. He was sweating and breathing hard, holding his chest.
Josh watched him from behind—he watched his back expand and

shrink in quick motions, trying to capture air with every strangled inhale, he was crying. He got up, using the tree as an aid.

"Let me get you help!" Josh said

"NO! I'm fine! Get help for your cousins!"

Walter pushed himself from the tree, staggering away, he seemed lost, confused and still holding his chest. His head is extremely pale, making the blood flowing from his wound look very bright. He fell to one knee, got up touching the blood running down his cheek, and then headed to his house across the street. Josh watched his frame distort from the heat waves that danced Jacksonville road.

Josh heard something that he will never, ever forget. From behind him, in unison he heard: "Hello, Joshua."

He turned in shock, standing there were Lily and Lilac! His mind went wild with confusion. He felt an evil fill his gut as the girls just looked at him smiling. They are not the same as they were before. Lily's hair is now jet-black; black as midnight, and Lilac's hair is pure white. They started to laugh! All he could do was run! However it did little good, in his head he heard them. "Run Josh run, run Josh run." Their voices ran through his mind, followed by laughter. He tried to cover his ears but it was useless. "YOU TELL, YOU DIE!" was the final message that swam his mind, over and over.

He ran towards his house, the laughter began to fade. Now it was only his heavy breathing that he heard—his own, thank God!

Something awoke in this town, something evil, and it's alive in his cousins.

Later that day, through the window of the second floor, from behind a curtain, Josh watched his aunt Marlow putting the girls in her car. "Can't she see the change?" Josh thought, but she was always oblivious to them. She never dared as long as the girls were occupied with something and out of her hair. And now, he didn't care either. They were leaving for a long weekend (According to his mother) and Josh was relieved.

That night, Josh couldn't sleep. He stared at the ceiling of his bedroom, watching the headlights of slow moving traffic from Jacksonville road, when suddenly he heard a noise. He looked out the window at the head of his bed and in the darkness, coming over the roof of his house, was a glowing, golden fog. He was dumfounded as he got up and went to the window in his room that had the porch-roof under it. He opened the window and could see the wonderful fog just drifting around the window. He thought heaven was falling, and then with unknown nerve, at first hesitant, he went out on the porch roof.

The roof stretched from the side of the house all the way to the front, bending right, extending the length of it. The shingles were still warm under his feet from yesterday's heat wave making the dew from the chill off night a little slippery.

Something strange is going on in the front of the house. The golden fog is drifting over the top of the shingles, looking like a golden stream flowing off the roof. Josh turns the corner and sees a bright golden light coming from Walter Smiths house. Not at the house, but behind it in the old apple orchard that Josh played in when he was younger. He can see little flares and pulses in the soft light, and the music, the music was surely angelic. Josh knew that the light was for Walter. He knew after today that he would never see him again, and this vision strengthens that feeling. This was not at all shocking to him; somehow this was allowed to be seen. Joshua was invited to an event that, most likely, many people were not allowed too see. Why he was allowed will remain a mystery. But he knew, after tonight, Walter Smith was gone, and ever since that August day, Towaco has never been the same.

* * *

Joshua realized he was staring into a blank television set. He still has his coat on and is wheezing badly. He feels hot; his head is burning, sweating, and he is tired. His ears are clogged with what seems like paste, it's difficult to hear. The doctors said not to over do it, but seeing his cousins again made his heart pound. He felt dizzy as he went to the kitchen to make sure the door was locked, and then headed up to his bedroom. It was only seven thirty in the evening, but he couldn't keep his eyes open any longer. Barely making it upstairs, he hears a television on in one of the bedrooms. The Magic Garden was playing on the black and white, with Petey and his mother both sleeping on her bed. He went to his room falling on his pillow. He was out before hitting it.

* * *

Josh woke to a noise outside his window. He knew it was late, but couldn't tell what time it was because he forgot to wind the old alarm clock on his dresser. He guessed it was after midnight on Saturday, but time seemed suddenly irrelevant. Because from the dead of night, a strange sound is calling him to the window at the head of his bed.

Outside his window there was a slight dusting of snow, and the clouds that brought it are long gone with a full moon taking over for the atmospheric dominance of the night sky. Everything is white, shimmering and beautiful. Josh lost himself for a moment looking at the wondrous world just outside his window. It was something out of a Dickens novel for sure and he is lost in its mystery. It was like looking at a dream—a beautiful dream. He cracked the window to breath in its chilly reality, it was cold on his lips and in his lungs, but it was like a jolt of spearmint in his mouth, exhaling its chill, fogging the windowpane.

Josh began coughing violently. Trying not to wake Petey, who somehow made it back to his bed when he was sleeping. Josh buried his face in his pillow. His little brother stirred a bit, and then turned on his side into shadows, sound asleep. That's when he heard that noise again, bringing him back to the reason why he was up in the first place. It's the sound of an airplane engine circling over the house. It wasn't a loud, annoying sound; it was quiet, steady, and rather soothing, just a single engine airplane drifting the clear, chilly night.

There are two known airports in this area and one is the Towaco Airport that is long abandoned for fifteen or twenty years now—and Lincoln Park Airport, which is still active, but about five miles away. This plane sounds too low for a landing in the latter.

Josh was beaming with curiosity. Even though Lincoln Park was still active with daily flights, no airplane ever flew at night. Though it must be a beautiful site, up high in the chilly air, however it was just never done. Many times Josh and Petey and other kids of Jacksonville road would camp out along the creak, behind the old barns—away from the houses, away from annoying parents, absorbing the mysteries of the night. They would lay awake under the stars in the summer nights of July and August, catching the shooting meteors and just gaze into the many stars drifting the heavens. It cannot be described how beautiful those nights were. And never once, had they ever seen a small engine plane so late at night.

Then, looking out his window, tilting his head in a position that he could barely breathe, he sees it. It came from the side of the house and around in the light of the moon. It was a biplane! It had no lights, except for a few sparks that came from the engine. It was dark, you can't see what color it is because shadows consumed it, but you can see it, drifting in the sky. I must be dreaming he thought, rubbing his eyes, trying to muffle his excitement, trying not to wake his brother. But it was a thrill any young boy would enjoy.

This was no dream, adrenalin running through him, watching the biplane drift in the moonlight was as soothing as the engine itself. The engine puttered as it disappeared behind the house. "It was going to land!" Josh said aloud, covering his mouth after blurting it out. Petey just stirred a little in the darkness then was silent.

Josh didn't know what to do. His body was busting with energy from the chilly air of the window and the excitement of the biplane. His breathing was hard and steady, lying in bed, wondering what to do. Should I go see? He thought. YES!

Josh rose on his arms, trying not to ruffle the bed, sat up grabbing his clothes, tiptoeing out the door to the hallway. The flash of light coming from the front bedroom stopped him. He heard Ralph Kramden bellowing obnoxious verbs from the black and white TV flickering in the doorway. He waited patiently for the punch line, and then slid down the railing, silently, in a flash of laughter.

Josh dressed in the hallway that wraps around the foot of the staircase. There are two ways to the kitchen in this old house. At the bottom of the stairs you ether make a right or a left. Going left brought you through the sitting room and the foyer that is big and empty, where nothing can hide to eat young kids. Or, you can make a sharp right through the dark hallway that passes the cellar door. No one ever went this way, too damn scary. It's dark by the cellar door and the perfect place for privacy, or, just to hide. He stares at the door not blinking while he dresses. It is old and beaten, weak from holding back the many demons that manifested

from a kids imagination that ran wild over the years. Just looking at it in the shadow of the stairs sends chills up his spine, but he
won't be here long and sure enough, moments later, he was done.
In the kitchen by the door, he pets the deaf dog with reassurance
that everything is all right, then slips his boots on.

Josh slipped out the door with ease. Stepping into the fluid of
moonlight is like stepping out on a stage of another world. The
light bouncing off the moon is lighting his world. Josh waves his
hand in the alien light and is utterly amazed how wonderful being
alive really is.

Josh looks at his aunt's house next door. It stops him cold as he
stares at it through the steam coming out of his hot lungs. It sits
tall and dark, under the oak tree towering over it, swaying in the
moonlight. It's even more frightening then the cellar door inside
his house. It's always dark—you never see more than one light
on, and since they found his uncle's body half outside the coal
furnace—dead, Josh never goes in the house. The last time he did
was for the funeral. The smell of burnt flesh still reeked through
the whole house, it was horrible. In the early days of coal burning houses the heating vent, for this house anyway was right in the
middle of the living room floor. It was three foot by three foot and
straight down to blackness. Josh stood over the grate, feeling the
hot air and burnt uncle coming up hitting him in the face. Something caught his eye, he remembers trying to focus, and suddenly
he had seen him, good God it was him. Standing over the grate,
looking down into the heating duct built right into the floor, he had
seen him. An incandescent, silhouette looking up at him in silent
agony—his uncle was staring from the blackness of the grate. He
ran and never, ever went back in the house!

The sound of the plane grabbed his attention once more. Forgetting his thoughts, and before he knew it, he was past the house that

haunted him so. He flew by it so fast it made his eyes tear. The cold was crisp against his cheeks, running with his arms wide, slicing the early morning November air, staring into the night sky as he ran through the dusting of powdered snow. The moonlight was thick—it felt like cold liquid on his body, making him feel so alive. He caught the biplane disappearing behind the old barns, its motor echoing off the rotten walls that has long since housed sheep, cows and strange-looking farm machinery. He ran as fast as he possibly could to the distant, dark silhouettes that lingered at the edge of the airfield and his grandfather's property. He zigzagged through the relics till he came to the last and biggest. He looked up at the massive wall before him, touching the frail, splintering wood that is brittle to the touch, feeling the history soaked deep into its fiber, it seems alive, a haunting feeling indeed.

He climbed the old stairs to the hayloft. This is what it was always called anyway, even though the loft hasn't stored hay in many years. As long as Josh could remember, it held old, forgotten furniture. Over the generations this barn collected the unwanted things his relatives parted with but refused to throw away, slowly building to an old antique shop that no one in the town of Towaco ever knew about.

Josh moved on, through the conglomeration of knickknacks and furniture, an eerie décor unfolding around him. There is a great opening in the back of the barn that was used to hoist large bales of hay up into it. Josh cannot see the opening, but the moonlight is shining off the old, crane-looking device hanging from the ceiling just at its entrance. He does not ever remember seeing it work but you can tell, even in the light of the moon shining on its old and tired gears, it was a powerful tool for a farmer in its day. Finally, coming around a huge bookshelf, it was like coming out of the dark woods into an open field, this was the opening of the loft.

The moon drenched him in a soft, blue light as he stood in the gaping maw, overlooking the old abandoned airport of Towaco. It was dizzying to look out over the vast runway with overgrown vegetation sprouting the black tar. Not to mention the old tires and rocks that hide under the foliage. That's when Josh realized there could be serious problems if he tries to land—in fact, he can't land. It will surely be a disaster.

The biplane came in view from the side of the barn. Josh can see it clearly in the moonlit sky. The purring of the engine tells him there are no troubles and no need for the plane to land, except maybe for the fact of low fuel.

As the plane flew by, he can see two heads sticking out of the fuselage. "Boy, they must be cold" Josh said to no one, shivering, feeling the chill of winter biting his nose.

After a moment, the biplane began to climb straight up into the night sky, turning wing over wing. It seemed it was going to disappear in the stratosphere, and suddenly when it was almost out of sight, it fell to one side and began spinning to earth. Round and round it spun with a tail of smoke coming from it. Faster and faster the plane shot to earth with the engine screaming in pain. He cannot believe this is happening in his sullen, small town. Just as he was ready to jump from the loft and run to get the fire department or anyone for that matter, Joshes eyes went wide, and long without blinking. The late November wind reminded him its time to do so, when he wiped the tears away, the biplane began to pull up. The stress on the engine eased and the plane flew level momentarily then went into a loop—slowly rising to etch out a circle in the night sky. But when it was completely upside down, at the top of its loop, the biplane began to glow. It did not seem to be in any kind of trouble; at least no sounds depicting trouble, actually it was a soothing, incandescent, alien glow. At first, Josh thought it was the moonlight playing tricks off the planes sides. It wasn't, the plane itself was glowing, and that was not the end of this enigma, as it came down in its three o'clock position, it started to emanate a glittering trail. Like the after effects of fireworks—a lovely tale of stars coming off the plane. It was mesmerizing!

Josh sat in the opening awestruck. He sat holding the old beam of the hayloft doorway, feet dangling over the side. His hands are cold, snot running down his face. He paid it no mind, he could not take his eyes off the event happening, the magic he was experiencing in the night sky.

For the next fifteen minutes or so, the plane would display wonderful aerobatics never experienced by Josh in his life time. It twisted and turned in ways he never thought possible. He just sat there his eyes drifting with the plane, grinning ear to ear, watching the glowing plane with its star-trail following it through the thick fluid of moonlight. Then something unexpected happen, Josh knew this would have to end, he didn't want it to, but all good things end, and after its wonderful display, he knew it would probably just drift off into the night. But that didn't happen.

As the plane leveled off, the person in the front exited the seat and was now walking on the wing. Josh stood immediately. Now, not only the tail of the plane had a streak of stars, so did the person on the wing. The stars bleeding out of this person were glittering soft pastels and different colors that were beautiful. As the plane circled the end of the airport where the abandoned hangers are, he or she let go. Falling slowly and softly, floating down through the air on the moonlight with the trail of colored stars following. Slowly descending down, just drifting in little circular motions, slower and slower until he or she floated behind the tree line. The biplane, after dropping off its passenger, began to dim. The star trail stopped emanating and the plane just grew dimmer as it flew

north, finally blinking out completely, like a candle going out from
a sudden wind, disappearing in the night. However, off in the
distance, by the abandoned hangers, there was something glowing,
something stayed behind—something not of this world.

Somewhere a door slammed behind him in the darkness. It
was the very one he came through on the other end of the barn.
The sound ran up his spine as he turned into darkness. He was so
awestruck by the biplane riding the moonlight that he didn't pay
any attention to the converted hayloft that now houses old furniture
from generations past. Was this the thing from the biplane? He
turned to the horizon; the glow was intense, illuminating the sky.
No he thought—it can't be.

His eyes started to adjust to the darkness, with images starting
to form. Dank smells of old furniture began to enhance the images of the hayloft. The first thing that forms for his adjusting eyes
is an old spindle. It once spun yarn, now it just silently collects
cobwebs. Now, his vision forms a maze of old dressers and china
cabinets. He looks into—

"Hello Joshua" Two voices spoke in harmonic, sadistic overtones. "We were waiting for you to come home."

Josh is glued to the side of the eighteenth century china cabinet. Lily and Lilac! They were his cousins all right, but the voices
were something other.

"Josssshhhuuuaaaa…" echoed once more through the hayloft. It
was heavy in his mind, like finger nails on a chalkboard.

Josh is frozen with fear. He glares around the corner to look down
the long path to the large opening of the barn stretching out to his
freedom, then to the back corner of the doorway leading to the
stairs. The door was a couple of feet away, so that was his first
option. The phlegm in his throat from a moldy atmosphere won't
go down. His breathing becomes heavy and hard, he hears the

patter of tiny steps echoing different parts of the loft. Grabbing the ice-cold doorknob, it doesn't turn. It's freezing out and somehow Josh manages to sweat profusely. His eyes are wide from hearing a draw opening somewhere in the forest of old wooden fixtures. Something dropped from the ceiling and landed on his shaved head, falling to his ear. He shook violently and ran down another path of square angles and protruding wood. Just as he got out of the way, a loud thud came from where he was standing. He can't see what it was, but he knew it wasn't good. Car headlights ran across the wall through the opening. Unnatural shadows moved in those lights and Josh ran down another dusty path. Going through cobwebs eased him a bit knowing that he is the first to pass through this way in years. He finds a table covered with a cloth and old boxes, he takes refuge under it. He crawls to the far corner against the wall, eating and wearing the many spider webs under it. He hears creaks from the floor boards, whispers flying back and forth. At present a new sound, thud—shhht, thud—shhht! Over and over, thud—shhht, thud—shhht. The sound he heard many times before from his grandfather chopping red, bloody carcasses. A meat cleaver hitting wood then pulled out, over and over, slow and steady, tormenting.

"Jooooshuaaa, come out, someone wants to meet you."

Silence, quiet, lasting only moments before whispers shot back and forth through the darkness of the barn, echoing the walls. Josh tries to pinpoint the voices, but they seem to be coming from everywhere.

"Oh, never mind scaredy cat, He will find you!"

Josh was frozen under the table. He couldn't move a muscle, fear is eating him alive. He tried not to breath, scared that what was with his cousins would see the hot steam coming from his lungs. Suddenly he heard a strange sound, but it was not the meat cleaver

this time. It was a dropping of a foot, then the drag of the other.
Josh sees a little flap in the cloth hanging off the table, he moves
slowly, trying not to make the floorboards creek. He slowly pulls
the flap and sees something however he can't make it out. Another
car slowly passes the bend of Jacksonville road. Once again headlights illuminate the room and he sees what is making the noise.
The shadow of a monster fills the headlights of a passing car. A
huge outline of its body covers the wall then melting away as the
car drifts away up the road. Everything went dark. Josh sees nothing, letting the flap drop, as he crawls back to his corner against
the wall. He hears the dragging of the foot and whispers echoing
all around the barn. He covers his ears, yet he still hears them. He
knows now they are in his head, it is not audible at all, some sort
of chant, over and over running through his mind. A sort of paralysis is coming over him, the chant was louder, and the presence of
something horribly cold close by. He can hear it's breathing, loud,
horrible, sickening breathing. From under the table, Josh can see
the oak-sized leg stop where the cover is half off. He can't move,
can't scream, he just stares at the shredded blue jeans of a deformed leg, as the chanting of his demonized cousins fill his head
more and more. He can't concentrate, it's taking over, his body is
numb, he can't move. Suddenly something was getting his attention—pulling him back from this strange paralysis. A howl in the
back of his mind, under the chanting torment, slowly it was getting
louder, distracting him from the rhythmic sound of the voices. The
fog of this trance begins to lift. He snapped his head and realized
what is was, it was something he hasn't heard in years. It was
Champ! It had to be years since he heard that howl of his dog.
It washed out the transfixing sound of the girls and brought him
back to his dilemma. And that's when he started to scream! He
screamed at the top of his lungs, as he watched the legs of the beast

jerk from being startled. The chant broke to a muffled whisper, but it only made matters worse.

The tarp suddenly flew off the table. The limping beast fell to one knee. Josh stared into the eyes of his worst nightmare. Its hair was wild and its face so horribly scared, twisting with the shadows, Josh couldn't take his eyes off it. Dressed in a torn dirty flannel shirt, hovered in front of him like a Mac truck, all Josh could do is scream, if he was going to die, the whole town of Towaco was going to know about it! The ugly bastard was reaching for him under the table. Josh kicked and screamed, but the monster easily had him by the ankle, dragging him out from under his shelter like a sack of potatoes. Dirt and dust was kicking up, getting into his eyes and mouth as he was being dragged through the maze of furniture, his shirt riding high up his back, becoming a pin cushion for splinters. He hears Champ howling like a mad wolf and the girl's frantic whispers back and forth to each other about it. He is whipped around a corner, hitting his head on the old freezer, sending white flashes in front of his eyes, with a searing pain shooting through his temple. The dragging stopped for the moment and he was looking up trying to focus on the shadows that made up the ark of the roof. Dust and dirt was falling into his mouth and eyes, making it hard to see. He was dazed, as the images of his cousins appeared looming over him. Two evil grins were looking down, blending with the shadows above, one with white hair and the other with black. Light from the opening shimmered in the spit from his white haired cousin as it landed on the lid of his eye. "A kiss from the evil one!" She giggled, then turning to the monster and said: "Take him, before that damn dog wakes the dead!" The dragging began once more, heading to the gaping hole of the barn. Josh tried desperately to reach for something he could grab, but he couldn't get hold of anything, everything is flying by so fast.

The beast was in full stride to the opening that stretched out to the sky. The opening was like a picture frame around the enormous bastard, and he was its center, and without breaking stride, he just walked off the second floor of the hayloft. Josh hit his head and felt the fall in a dizzying whoosh, with a sudden smack across his back like being hit with a two-by-four. The lights suddenly went out. Only for a moment, the ache in his back brought him back from unconsciousness, with the help of the cold snow and muddy dirt on his back and neck. He tried getting his bearings but all he could see is flashes of night sky and the horrible beast in front of him. Josh began to cry. He didn't have to see, he knew where he was going—he was heading to the well. Images flooded his mind, he had seen its edge, he felt the cold cement that surrounded the opening, felt how smooth the cement formed the hole of the opening. He heard the beast's echoing breath bouncing around the cylindrical wall of the well. He sees himself being swallowed by the mouth of it, he feels the cold cement as he grabs for dear life, then the hole growing smaller as he falls into oblivion.

But he wasn't there yet. The wet, snow covered, soggy ground against his back told him so. Looking up at the sky in a daze, he can see the hot smoke of his breath obscuring the stars. This tells him he is still alive, but for how long?

His dog champ's distant howl was growing louder, bringing Josh out of a fading trance. He tried to twist and claw the ground, trying to grab anything that would help delay his descent into a nightmare. Weeds and mud slipping though his fingers, he could not grab hold however hard he tried, he wouldn't give up, he needed an anchor and he needed it now. The howl that echoed the night is growing louder turning into vicious barks and growls. Finally Josh felt the moss of an oak tree, and the hump of the roots from it, grabbing hold, hanging on for dear life! He can see the lights are now on in the kitchen of his house, far up the driveway. With the sudden stop, the monster lost his grip, letting out the most hideous cry of anger, sending a wave of frost up Josh's spine. The creature grabbed his legs and yanked hard, breaking his grip, coming back around swinging Josh like a baseball bat against the oak tree. A horrible thud was heard. Joshes body contoured and bent around the oak with a jolting flash in his eyes. The dragging began once more. Josh was in shock, his arms flailed spastically over his head like dead meat. He had no control of his body. He can only look at the specks of light gleaming through the branches of the oak. He can hear the barking getting closer. The brown shape of a blur suddenly came into view and consumed the figure dragging him. A whirl of growls and screams filled the growing darkness of Joshua Weaver's eyes. He stopped moving, his leg that was in tow with the monster thudded to the ground. He lifted his head to see Champ at his feet and the monster slipping into the well. Suddenly, all was quiet. His best friend lay next to him, putting his head on his chest, panting. Joshua can hear a frantic voice calling his name as his mother's silhouette came into view from the darkness. She looked pale, sick with anguish. She looks like a ghost. He could not keep his eyes open any longer, Joshua passed out...

Josh awoke to blurry silhouettes. Even though it was dark in the room with no lights on, it was light enough to see a blurry collage of abstracts dance the walls. The drip of an IV bottle was his first semi-focused image as things began to solidify around him. He was exhausted. He could only roll his head from side to side, rolling the obscure pictures on the white walls. He knows this reality all too well. The aroma of sanitation and disinfectant knots his stomach as things started to clear.

He is back at the hospital.

Hearing his name, he turned to a distorted but molding face; first it was three, then two, and one, it was his mother looking at him with tired eyes. One would think they were sad eyes but he knew she was just tired—maybe both. Yes, the remorse was there, but so was the intolerable, hard life that plagued her for years, right there in those tired eyes. Her lips, pale and dry, open to say something, but she doesn't, they close and knot with tears flowing. She looks away, towards the window, with her body following to see something, but all she could look at was her own reflection. One could only imagine what she sees.

Josh could see her fully in the window's reflection with her hands in a ball of crumpling and twisting agitation.
"Everyday I wait for that damn phone to ring." She said looking into the eyes of a tired woman. Josh could only stare at a mother who was weakening from troubles. She pushes back her messy hair, wiping tears away in the same motion.
"Every God damn day I pray that the next time it rings it would be for you. If we don't get a donor soon—" She turned towards him, stopping in mid-sentence, eyes red with irritation. "All I am going to say is you can't be going on midnight strolls with your fucked up, little cousins!"

Her mouth knotted once more, looking deep into his eyes. "Tell me, did those little bitches push you from the loft? If I find out they did I'll—"
"Son-of-a-bitch, Josh!"
She turned towards the window, tears flowing.
She doesn't know.
Josh was quiet. He wants to tell her everything. He wants to scream to the world what his cousins truly are. He wants to tell her there is evil coursing through their veins. How his evil cousins were able to put demonic thoughts through his mind. He wants her to know about the creature of the well—how this lunatic creature

lives and travels the sewers of Towaco. But he can't. She would never believe him, and if they knew she had an idea of what they were, what would they do to her? No! He can't take that chance. "I fell." He muttered, with tears welling up in his eyes. "I fell."

"Then what the hell were you doing out there in the middle of the God-damn night, Josh?"

As she spoke the biplane came flooding back to him. The beautiful glowing airplane was swirling and dancing in his mind once more. He was watching it fly and do loop-de-loops and just softly glitter against the night sky.

"Well?" brought his eyes back to his mother's glare.

"I wanted to see the stars." Josh said in a whisper.

"While I still can."

His mother covered her mouth, tears streaming down her face. She was backing up to the door looking at him like she found him dead in his bed, turning and running through it. Josh was sorry for what he said, but the questioning had to stop. Though his mother was searching, he couldn't take a chance of giving any info about his cousins in his present condition, or anything else that happened that night. He is tired, his head is heavy like a bowling ball, and so were his eyelids. Sleep started to echo his mind, it was calling, and he so graciously answered.

* * *

Joshua stood outside his second home, Riverside Hospital, looking into the late-winter sky when two nurses walk by and said hello. The staff at RH knows him by name, as if he were a fellow employee. He turned to see his mother talking to the doctor that took care of him behind the automatic sliding glass door. He was talking and she was nodding, looking out at Josh. After shaking hands, she came outside. She gave Josh a soft smile, putting her arm around him with a gentle hug, as they headed across the parking lot. The seventy-two, white Plymouth sat in a lone slot under an elm far on the other side of the hospital. It was covered with snow and the handle was freezing to his fingers. This car has been sitting here for days. Josh thought, and suddenly realizing his mother stayed, she never left.

"Where's Petey?" He said, knowing the answer, but trying to break the bleak silence of a dismal winter day.

"He stayed with grandma, but we have to get him from kindergarten now."

"Can I go to school tomorrow?" He asked.

"Monday" She said, looking at him. "It's Friday afternoon." Joshes is taken back, he lost all sense of time. He knew he was in the hospital a couple of days, but had no idea it was over a week. His mother, seeing his confusion, said:

"You were asleep for the first three days. Now help me get this crap off the windshield."

Josh did, helping remove the leave sand the light snow that fell from his side of the car.

The leather of the seat was cold, stiff and uncomfortable. When the engine finally fired up after a few attempts, a blast of cold air blew from the vents sending pieces of leaves, dirt and dust through the whole car. They sat there holding themselves, rubbing their arms. Josh look at his mother and said:

"Thanks for staying with me mom." He smiled at her. She grabbed is head, kissed it, and said: "let's go get your brother."

The car finally felt warm as they pulled into their driveway. Petey was bouncing in the back seat from the excitement of being with his brother and finally having him home. The first thing Josh did was to look and see if his cousins were around. They weren't. His aunt's car was nowhere to be seen. He felt a little easy now when his mother said they went to Tarrytown, NY for a week, visiting a relative Josh did not know. He felt at ease, he can rest before the possessed bitches return. However there is something much more than just his fucked up cousins acting strange, something far worse, something that had Josh by the ankle, dragging him to the mouth of the well.

Towaco was chilly this night. The fire made cracking sounds as his mother threw another log on the fire. She sat back staring into the ambers. Josh watched a flickering haze of orange cover her eyes. She put Petey's sleeping head back on her lap.
"Wow, its only 9:30 and Petey is out." Josh said.
His mother sighed. "He must have caught a bug from grandma, she is always coming down with something."
Josh turned back to the fire. Not thinking of any one thing, but a collage of images of the biplane that drifted the sky the other night. As the conversation trailed off, Josh went to the big picture window in the living room. It was hard to look out into the night because the glow of the fire dancing in the window, but he can still see the dark shape of the house next door. He can see the white of the snow spreading out in all directions, leading up to the dark tree line deep in the back of the house. He turned from the window and yawned. He could barely keep his eyes open, he decided to go up to bed.

Josh woke to an elusive feeling. The wind up now said twelve thirty-five. Josh stared at the ceiling of his room, knowing, instantly something was going on. There was a strange chill touching his neck from the window where his head laid. He felt it many times before but this time it was different. It was cold, yes, but ever so soothing. It didn't just nip at his neck, but caressed it. As comfort-

ing as it was, it still made his hair stand frigid. He snaps his head
to the window, looking out the frosted window pane.

There, through the dew-laden glass, was an amazing sight. Out
passed the yard, beyond the dead garden, just behind the thick tree
line, was a lavender blue glow. Josh knew the spot immediately.
Something inside his gut told him, it was Herman's pond. Herman's pond is a personal sanctuary deep in the woods. It's known
only to a few locals and is a great place to ice skate in the winter.
There is only one, easy way to it, and that is to follow the stream
from the drain pipe that snakes through his grandfathers' farm,
crawling through the foliage of the woods.

Josh's eyes were wide. He wiped the wet dew from the window
so he could see the aura glowing over the trees. He didn't know
what to do. His chest heaved with excitement, yet there was no
way he is going there tonight. Yet he can't stop thinking about the
person who exited the bi-plane. The beautiful vision is ever so
vivid in his mind. Whoever it was, floated down on a bed of stars,
falling behind the tree line on swirling shimmers of light. The
image is so real he can feel the chill through his body. He pulled
the blanket up to his shoulders and just stared out over his back-
yard, out passed his garden to the alien glow emanating through
the forest. Somehow, whatever is out there knows he will not be
coming tonight. Josh felt totally relaxed, watching the top of black
trees sway in and out of the glowing aura. His sickly condition is
making him tired, and he needs his rest. Even though his body is
chilled with delight, his face is warm. He knows this feeling all to
well, if he looks into a mirror, he will see a yellow faced boy looking back at him. However looking will only be a waste of time.
His liver is truly haunting him, there is no obvious pain, however
something just below his ribcage that feels slightly swollen. He
feels the toxins rising in him with a warm feeling that is unexplain-

able. As his eyes grow heavy, the glow outside his window begins to slowly pulse with shimmers of light starting to drift towards the house. He watches the gentle lights, like silver lightning bugs with blue trails, millions of them, coming through the woods. His eyes get heavier and heavier with the wave of shimmers now reaching the back yard, and seconds later engulfing his house. If this were another time, Josh would be ecstatic, but not tonight. His liver won't allow it. It will not let him enjoy this miracle touching his home. There is nothing to do but sleep on it.

This stay at Riverside was short. Two days is nothing to Josh. The doctor can't believe how well he recovered this time. "It's hard to believe that two days ago you were piss yellow with your eyes rolling back in your head." The young doctor said, scratching his ear with a ballpoint pen. "You have a strong immune system my friend or, you were touched by an angel. But anyhow, you are going home and I want you to rest." Josh knew this man for a long time, remembers him as an intern, the doctor who never combs his hair, but always has a soft comforting smile.

Driving home, Josh stared at Towaco floating by his eyes. He stared at the different houses and churches that seem to never end. His mother said nothing. She has a meeting with Dr. Gilda and that was consuming her thoughts. Josh forgot all about it. Petey is at Grandma's and his mother will be gone all afternoon. His mind ran wild. He has two maybe three hours to do some exploring in the woods of the abandoned airport. His eyes were wide with anticipation. His mother sensed something as she turned into the driveway of their house, her brows arc as if to try and figure out what was rolling in his mind. She doesn't know what, but she is suspicious, you can say mother's intuition.

The old Plymouths door made a popping noise as it opened, with a long squeak to follow. The chilly air instantly turning his breath to smoke, it is a chilly, gray afternoon.

He ran with new vigor to the back door, he has a lot of planning to do before his trip to the abandoned airport. He needs to find his boots and—

His little trip will be delayed. Josh nearly jumped out of his skin when he saw the person sitting there in the dark of the kitchen. He tried to focus his eyes from the sudden light-change of the room, trying to focus on the outlined shadow sitting at the end of the kitchen table. A glowing trail of a cigarette illuminated a wrinkled face in the shadows as white smoke filled the cracks of her face. He knew the features all too well. His eyes focused and watched the smoke tangle with her wild hair. It was Gretchen—old Gretchen Woodbury. After the sound of hissing smoke from her lungs, a raspy voice greeted him. "Well, hello, Josh."

He just stared at the old woman. The screen door screeched open and his mother was next to him. Josh didn't even turn to see his mother walk in. He just watched the light reflecting from the movement of the door dance across Gretchen's wrinkled form. His mother touched his shoulder. "I thought it would be a good idea to have someone sit with you while I was out." She said with a solemn voice.

He knew it was a lie. She didn't trust him, and with good reason. After the other night, telling her tales of watching stars late at night, he can somewhat understand. Yes he should demand her trust, but for now, to protect her and his brother, he must let it go. "The doctor said you are to rest, and that is what you will do." She said, fanning the cigarette smoke from her face, shooting a look at Gretchen.

Josh couldn't take his eyes off the old woman. She lived alone and he had barely ever seen her, only in the darkness of her windows and screened doors when he would pass her house, never seeing her outside during the day, and if she did go out it was rare, mostly always at night. Many times Josh would watch her from the edge of the garden near the road. He watched her push the lawn mower in darkness, working the old rake that always stood by her side door. He guessed, she must sleep during the day. It was eerie watching her silhouette against the darkness, with fireflies softly glowing around her on hot summer nights. She was called the Witch of Jacksonville Rd. Her husband Bud, was the postman for many years, one of three in Towaco; he's been dead for years, after he died she stopped going anywhere.

Josh stared at the black sacks that hung from under her eyes, holding up her blood filled yellow puss pockets that her irises floated in. She smirks at his curiosity, taking another drag of her cigarette, not taking her eyes off him, while he sat across from her with a confusing stare.

"I was getting the mail the other day and I ran into her. We chatted a bit and she said she would love to sit with you while I am gone."

"Now Gretchen, if there is anything you need, just ask Josh." His mother said, rubbing her nose from the smoke.

Gretchen just gave her a little smile and a nod.

With a long stare his mother looked hard at Josh. "You be good, I'll see you later."

He turned to her without saying a word, and watched the door slam, watching the broken pieces of his mother through the window panes of the back door.

Josh turned once more to Gretchen. She was looking at him while slightly tossing her pack of L&M cigarettes with her left hand. Josh broke his stare, noticing her ashtray was already full with cigarette butts. He grabbed it, headed to the garbage. "Have you been waiting long, Mrs. Woodbury?"

"A while, give or take. She said, smirking. Yes I do smoke an awful lot."

Josh swallowed hard. He didn't know what to say. Her intuitiveness caught him off guard, as if she was reading his mind. She broke the tension finally saying: "Come sit down Josh, we need to talk."

She grabbed another cigarette, after lighting it added: "Turn on the fan over the stove; it will help with the smoke."

Josh did as she asked, then sat next to her nearest to the stove.

The kitchen was one big cloud of smoke. The smell of sulfur from the wood-stick matches she used also filled the air. It was an unpleasant combination of odors indeed, but somehow it only bothered him a little. He was lost in this old woman, mesmerized by how horrible one person can get just by letting yourself go. She emanated an alien radiance that is just unexplainable—yes she was horrible looking, but Josh can feel that she knows things, things that no one else knows.

Gretchen took a long drag from her cigarette and then watched smoke blend around the light hanging over the kitchen table. "So, you ran into Craven." Josh's eyes went wide, looking at her in amazement. "You know him?" Josh yelled. "He tried to kill me! We should call—"Gretchen stopped him with one wave of her hand.

"Yes he's real, or, at least used to be. We can't call the police, because they won't do a thing."

She let out a deep sigh, looking at her pack of L&Ms. Josh sat there, slack jawed. "There must be something we can do!" Again, her commanding hand swam the air. "Nothing! Not from the law anyway"

He sat back, knotting his eyebrows with confusion. "Why?"

"I said he was real, I didn't say he was human, or natural. Many years ago, before you and your family moved back to your grandfather's farm, there was a terrible, terrible accident." She leans back in her chair, the most disgusting, mucus turning cough wailed from her long and hard, grabs another cigarette with her yellow fingers and again a matchstick flares to life. The smell of sulfur fills his nose once more, watching her go through what is now, after many years of repetition, natural to her.

"Craven Dune is who you met the other night, or what is left of him anyway. He wasn't the brightest boy, hell he was damn near retarded if you ask me, but that's neither here, there or Tuesday. Anyway, do you know the flood pipe that runs the length of Jacksonville road? It ends here behind the barns?"

"Yes, of course." He said.

"Well, years ago one spring it rained hard and heavy. It was a warm winter with very little snow. God decided to make up for it and in April the water works came. It just started to rain and wouldn't stop. People were worried that it was going to be a dry summer, huh! Dry it wasn't. April 1st it started, heavy downpours daily and didn't stop till the very end of May, to the day."

She took a long drag, continuing on the exhale.

"Craven was a pudgy, happy kid. He loved to play in puddles, boy I tell you, loved to get dirty."

She was staring into nothing, smiling as she thought of long ago. But her smile seemed to break, as the happy memories were suddenly overrun with the bad.

"Like I said, the rain was hard and heavy. Most kids were gloomy and miserable when they couldn't go out and play. However, a little rain never stopped Craven, in fact, he loved it, let me tell you. During the heavy rains the boy was in sheer heaven. I remember seeing him riding one of those bikes with the banana seat, wearing a rain coat and a rain hat that made him look like the

Morton's fisherman. It brought a smile to your face, it did." She took another long drag, Josh watched smoke float past her ear. The hum of the refrigerator kicked on. She continued.

"Finally, the rains stopped. The second the sun broke through the clouds the children of Towaco broke out their back doors, free of confinement, bursting into the light of day and suddenly the streets were full of kids playing and screaming. The town was alive again."

Gretchen took a long drag, closing her eyes in euphoric delight. The smell of burning, hot cigarette filter is heavy in the air. Her lungs wheezed, she coughed, smoke shot from her nose.

"Kids were in the parks, the softball fields—swings were flying high with kicking feet. They stayed far away from water as humanly possible because their souls needed to dry out from the dampness that swept the town for pretty near two months."

Something creaked in the living room of the old house, breaking the silence of heavy concentration. Josh rubbed his temple. It is hurting from not being able to take his eyes off Gretchen.

"Craven, on the other hand—was a different matter. He wasn't like other kids, the boy could not stay away from water, and after a few days of sunshine there were no puddles left for the boy to disrupt. So he went where there was a lot of it.

Up Jacksonville road, across the railroad tracks is the mouth of the basin, which is the opposite end of the drain pipe that ends here on the farm, opening up to the creak. Kids would laugh, because they would stand at the entrance of the pipe, hearing him playing little silly games. How he could go in that pipe alone was beyond me, but he would, I tell you, he would, brave kid he was."

She trailed off, her mind drifted and she seemed lost for a moment. She rubbed her thin, barely visible mustache under her bulbous nose and continued.

"Even though the rains stopped, Towaco would still flash flood from time to time. Jasper Mountain was relentless that year. We would hear it at night, sometimes, Bud and me. It sounded like a train running through the pipe that stretches under Jacksonville road from one end to the other. Bud would say 'it is sure to kill somebody, someday.' And he was right. One hot day, it came without warning, as it usually does, and Craven was in its hungry path. The kids that witnessed it said Craven just stared into its ferocity, he couldn't move, like a deer in headlights. After the sudden wave tumbled him, all they could see was an arm here, a head there, twisting and turning as if he was in a washing machine. His cries were muffled by dirty, mountain water filling his lungs. They saw his pudgy, little fingers hanging from the rim of the pipes' entrance as the water flushed through it. The next moment, they were gone. His screams echoed through the town, and no, they never found his body."

She sat back with a tear in her eye, maybe from sadness, maybe from all the smoke that is fogging up the kitchen. Her thoughts drifted different times from the past, her lip quivered slightly. Josh was about to say something, however he is at loss for words.

"Renina needs to see you." She said finally, not looking at him, just picking at her leathery cigarette stained fingers.

Josh said nothing. He never heard that name before, but somehow knew whom she was talking about.

"The person who fell from the plane?"

"Oh, my dear, she didn't fall, she drifts on star dust." She said, picking up her smoke once more, taking a deep inhale, and then putting it out in the ashtray.

"Is she human?"

"No."

"Not for a long time anyway."

He just looked at the old woman as she glared back into his eyes.

"If she's not human then—"

"She's an angel." She interrupted.

His heart was thick in his chest. He felt it swell, pounding in his throat, echoing in his ears, as he sat back glaring into nothing, just the rhythmic pounding of his heart keeps him from losing himself.

"Josh, you must go see her, tonight.

"Why can't I go now?"

"You can't see her by day. She glows too brightly to be seen in the daylight. You must go when it's dark, follow the glow. I know you have seen it; you must wait for the glow over the woods then go and see her. Listen to what she has to say, do exactly what she tells you." Gretchen trailed off, grabbing another smoke.

"How do you know all this?" He said, with watery eyes.

She again lit her cigarette, staring off to the kitchen windows, looking at the trees blowing in the wind.

"You, dear boy, are not the first one to be called. It started with my husband many years ago. That is when I became—aware.

The dancing of Renina is very old. The different seasons of death are greeted with different types of angels, I only know the winter angel—Renina, the ice dancer."

"Gretchen, when Walter Smith came out of the well trying to save my cousins, he died that night. There was an orange glow coming over the back fields of the apple orchard, was that—"

"Yes," She nodded softly with her eyes closed. "The angel of the second season—summer. But she missed him. He was not there when she came calling."

Josh looked puzzled. "I don't understand."

"You will."

His eyes suddenly went wide.

"I see it now! My sickness is killing me—I am going to die."

He just looked at her, hoping she would say something, to give him some kind of encouragement that everything would be all right, that she does not take everyone, but she didn't. Her eyes were glued on the wind-swept trees outside the window.

"She's here for someone, Josh, that's all I can say."

Josh's eyes began to well up with tears: "And what if I don't go?" He said.

Gretchen grabbed his hand softly: "When called, we go."

"I'll call the police, I'll—"

She cut him off.

"They can't see her, Josh, the living and the healthy cannot see her. Only the chosen ones and the dying can see what she truly is. When called, we go."

At that moment the kitchen door flew open. Joshes mother came in holding Petey in her arms. She looked tired and worried.

"What's wrong?" Josh said looking at his brother crumpled in her arms.

"Petey has a high fever, he's burning up." She said, paying no mind to Josh and Gretchen. "I'm going to put him to bed, bring me the aspirin." Josh nodded as she headed to the stairs. As Josh was getting up, Gretchen grabbed his arm saying in a whisper:

"You must go soon. Listen to her and be strong."

Josh said nothing, after a moment, he did as his mother wanted. He went to get the aspirin.

Up in the bedroom, Josh handed her the bottle. Petey lay under the covers. He can see his little head just barely out of the top of the covers.

"He's burning up." She said; busy tucking blankets and feeling his head.

"What happened?"

"When I got to Dr. Gilda's office there was a message from

grandma. She said Petey was sick, so I cancelled the appointment and went to bring him home." Josh looked at her with sad eyes. "So you didn't get a chance to talk to him?" He said, staring at his brother. His mother stopped working and shot him a troubling stare. "Why… no, Petey was sick, so I rescheduled for next week."

Josh said in a low voice that she couldn't hear: "It will be too late then!"

She seen his eyes were wet with tears. He turned from her and went to the window. He looked out into the cold day, choking back tears—tears of rage. He spoke with a slurred tongue: "So you didn't talk to him about a donor? Petey was more important?" She turned, looking at him. "You know that is not why I was going there. You know if there is a donor the hospital will call, it has nothing to do with Gilda! And if you must know the reason, it was to tell him I couldn't give him his monthly payment for your doctor bills. Grandma's call bought me—us a little more time." Josh turned to her expecting to see angry eyes, but they weren't angry at all, they were sad. She looked at him pushing her tired hair behind her ear. As she looked back and forth between the two boys she lost control and fell to the edge of the bed, crying. Her hands cupped her face and her sobbing overflowed her fingers. Josh was lost in the moment. He didn't want to hurt his mother. She works hard to keep the family somewhat sane and normal, but this is beginning to take its toll. He felt horrible for what he'd done to her. The only thing he could think of doing was to go to her, sit next to her, and hold her. They both sat there crying, holding each other with Petey's hot, sickly little body lay behind them asleep.

* * *

Later in the evening things were calm. Petey was feeling better and up playing with his trucks, while Josh sat in front of the picture window. He hears the sound of dishes being washed while he looks out into the darkness of the back yard. Earlier his aunt came knocking on the door. He heard verbal rhetoric being passed between her and his mother, so he knew the little bitches were home.

His mother didn't bring up the other night, he knows she didn't forget, couldn't forget, would never forget, but she is just too emotionally drained to consider a confrontation right now.

There is going to be trouble soon, but he doesn't care anymore. With death just over the trees passed the garden, it all seems irrelevant now.

He sits watching the trees blowing in the wind. Cold, wet, freezing rain hits the window in sheets, sending a chill through his body. He sinks deep into his chair, wrapped in its high arms. He pulls a checkered afghan that is part of the chairs ensemble around him and stares out the window.

Growing up in this town, he was always afraid of the dark, and this house especially used to frighten him. Lack of lights, always dim and dark, made it a scary place, but somehow, now he has changed. To him, the house is an enchanting place, a place to hide when his world becomes too overwhelming. So inviting, a place to lose ones self, lost in the crevasses of the welcoming unknown. Yes—Josh has changed. The darkness, now he realizes is a living entity. Just another creature that exists here on earth and it has every right to flourish and be wild. It's an awareness that is just so welcoming now, so hard to resist.

Josh was startled by a touch from his mother who was studying his intense stare at the pelting rain. She looked to see what was there, beyond the rain, but only dark silhouettes of nature and her own reflection looking back at her. Touching his shoulder she said:

"You should get ready for bed, please bring Petey with you."

"Ok, mom."

Josh grabbed Petey's hand. It was very warm and looking at him, he can tell he is still not well. His face was red with sickness, but he'll be OK. Petey always is, and the way he was playing with his toys, he is already on the way to recovery.

Upstairs, Petey jumped into bed. With his tired face he still bounced on the bed as children do. Josh sat across from him and was taking off his shoes. He was feeling tired, but knew he had to go to the woods tonight. Gretchen said: "When called you go." However he is not waiting to be called. He decided to go tonight, and that is what he is going to do. He got up and headed to the bathroom. He didn't know why he should bother brushing his teeth, I guess it's out of habit, or to kill time, nonetheless his teeth will sparkle with fresh breath for his party of demise. As he brushed, he noticed a soft light began glowing outside. He looked into the face of the full moon. The rains have ended, and now, to his surprise, the sky is clear, full of moon light.

When Josh came back into the room, he found Petey out of bed, up next to the window with the night looking back at him. This was out of character for the boy because he is scared of his own shadow. The room is dark, normally he wouldn't move until Josh, or his mother was there, however there he was, glued to the windowsill—absorbed by the night.

"Petey?" Josh said, looking at his little brother in the moonlight. Petey turned with half his face slipping into the shadow of the room, said nothing, turning back looking out into the cold, winter night. Josh walked over to the window to see what had his attention. Out over the garden, a faint glow began to pulse over the tree line. It's not as bright yet, Josh knew, being that its only half past ten, but it will get stronger as the night goes on.

"Petey, go back to bed." Josh said, but he didn't move, he just kept looking out over the tree line. His eyes drooping as he just stared out the window. Josh finally sat on his bed, watching the moonlight illuminate his little brothers' face.

"What does she want?" Petey finally said.

Josh was taken back, thoughts were running through his mind. How does he know? He wasn't home when he was talking to Gretchen, frankly, he was too sick to even notice her. But somehow, he knows.

"Who, Petey?"

"The woman who dances on ice, I watched her dance in my dreams. She would help me sleep when I couldn't. She is real nice, but she dances with people, and then takes them into the stars."

Josh sat back on his bed in deep thought. He can't believe what he is hearing. Josh thought about what Gretchen said, only the pure at heart can see her, but she said nothing about little boy's dreams.

"She would tuck me in, give me kisses on my head, and giggle."

"Petey," Josh said with a burning look. "Does she have a name?"

Petey turned to him and nodded with a half face of moonlight.

"Renina."

Josh didn't know what to say, sitting back in the shadows of the window.

Petey suddenly snapped. "Don't you dance with her! She'll take you to the stars. Then I will never see you again!"

Petey's eyes began to well with tears. Josh comforted him as best he could, reassuring and promising that he will not dance with her. Petey's hands balled up into little fists and he started to cry. He just sat there and held him. There was nothing more to say.

Josh put his brother back on his own bed. He was asleep just moments after telling him about the ice dancer and little fragmented details of what she was doing. Petey was nervous because he never thought she was real, even though he did not see her here in reality, he knows she is out there, calling people to the stars. Josh just looked at the soft glow over the tree line, he felt calm looking into the pulse of light. He knows the calling will be for him, he does not know when, but he will find out tonight.

Josh woke from a drifting nod. The glow from the woods was bright. It was so bright it looked like an incandescent fog flowing through the trees, seeping from the main glow further back in the forest. It was so beautiful that it was hard to look away. He glanced at the old wind-up clock on his dresser, half passed twelve, he looked at Petey, it took a minute for his eyes to adjust from the bright glow outside, but he's there, lost in a deep sleep. Josh turned back to the window.

"Its time to go." He whispered.

Once again he heard the familiar "To the moon, Alice!" coming from his mothers TV. He listened for any strange movement, but none was heard. Down the bannister once again he slid slowly, feeling the heat build from the friction of gripping it too hard to keep a slow descend, dismounting, go past the cellar door, then to the kitchen. He turned one last time, listening for any movement coming from upstairs—there was none. The sound of a tail thumping the floor got his attention; it was champ lying in the corner, excited as he can possibly get for an old dog. However he did not get up, he has had enough excitement for one week—telling Josh with droopy eyes that he is on his own tonight.

He opened the door and slipped through with not so much as a sound. The air was white and cold, instantly fogging his breath. Yes he felt the chill of December but that didn't seem to bother him much now. It is so dark; yet the world seems illuminated, almost glowing. He's suddenly drawn to the many stars glimmering in the chilly night sky, watching them pulse in the darkness. He looked from east to west, a sea of shimmering stars touching horizon to horizon—breathtaking is the only thought in his mind, as he walks while staring into the night.

Reality of night came flooding back to him when he heard his aunt's house creak and moan. The house is alive he thought, not haunted. It just sits in its own darkness, drab and dreary, like it's trying to hide from the wonderful moonlight. The house has an odor he never noticed before, it reeks of evil, and what he sees as he comes around the corner, in the basement window just above ground, proves true to his beliefs.

The whole house is dark, just a black silhouette in the night except for the basement window it is lit with a yellow light. Josh looks up at the window of his aunt's bedroom where a black and white television fills the room with the different intervals of light and shadow of late-night TV. Josh's eyes move with caution to the basement window and he sees the single light bulb hanging from the ceiling. He feels a sudden chill not associated with the conditions from the outside environment, something from the house was frightening him. He has come to realize that this house does not belong here. It's a cancer infesting the body of a beautiful world. And on the floor of that basement he sees the cause of the infectious reality inside that house—his cousins. Lily and Lilac are busy doing something on the cold, concrete floor. He watches Lilac busily at the foot of the overflowing coal bin, drawing something that looked like a giant circle with a piece of the black coal, while Lily stood over her, rocking back and forth, her lips were moving but he couldn't make out what she was saying. The hanging light over them began to move with the rocking of his cousin—Josh decided they were busy doing something, and while they were occupied, it was time to go. He turns and heads to the barn off in the distance illuminated by the moonlight.

The happenings of the other night came flooding back into his mind. He sees the well with its newly built cover, his mother hired a handyman and he did a fine job, Josh can smell the fresh paint still lingering the air, and he sees the many cinder blocks sitting on top. This is not going to keep that bastard from hell in, but it will keep people from falling down. He knows it has many exits, he knows the thing runs and lives in the drains of Jacksonville road, there are many ways to the surface, but seeing this makes Josh feel a little better.

Josh stands above the five-foot round flood pipe that opens up to a wide ditch running deep into the woods of Towaco. He loses himself staring at the water coming out of the pipe, the moonlight swims in the moving current, making the water glisten with sparkles as it rolls by. The sound it makes is oh, so soothing as he watches it disappear into the darkness. He looks off into the horizon of the tree line. The sky over the woods was a beautiful purple lingering in one area he knows well—Herman's pond. And this dark, deep ditch is the only way there.

Josh walked the edge above the ditch, walking the sides until the foliage was too thick to go any further. Where the foliage is thickest, this is where a path begins down into the trench.

Josh looks at the glistening, flowing stream running off into the woods. He looks up at the roughly fifteen-foot clayish-sandy walls that climb both sides. Everything is covered in moonlight, making it easy to see the different landscapes and forms that were sculpted from the flowing water. Right now it's a gentle flowing stream, but when the waters are high from the sudden flash flooding that happens quite often here in Towaco, it could become a flowing hell. That's why the walls are so high, from the massive floods digging deeper into the earth. Josh is overtaken by the sullen beauty of it all. He inhales deep, cold air. He is alive, so wonderfully alive.

Then in an instant, the euphoria that consumed him shattered. A long scream echoing the drainpipe sent a sharp chill up his spine. Sleeping birds took flight from the horrible sound that drifted the cold, night. He turned to the mouth of the pipe that is long off in the distance. Its opening is hidden from the moonlight, making it hard to see in the distance. He heard running, heavy footfalls splashing the stream inside the pipe, echoing the black hole in front of him. Heavy, hard breathing also was heard bouncing the pipe walls, another scream made Josh want to hide, but he couldn't move. He just stood there vulnerable in the cold night, shivering at the black hole of hell far off in the distance. He knew what it was; it was Craven from the other night. The scream he does not remember, but the heavy breathing flooded his mind with horror, how he was dragged through the wet, snow and mud. "No not again!" He said low, to himself. He covered his ears, shaking his head in a lunatic manner, not again. Then a sight he could not believe made his heart pound. Above the black pipe, stood the horrid creature, just a black silhouette lurched over the hole. He sees the beast above yet he can still hear the running foot falls in the pipe, growing louder. Josh's mind ran with fear—there are two of them! But something was not right. He can hear the frantic activity from the beast within the hole, but the one outside, was somber. Just standing over the entrance, the only movement was its heavy breathing. The creature, inside was louder. Josh knew he turned the wide angle of the pipe from the street, and is in direct line for getting him. He could hear the excitement of the beast, Josh can't see him, but he knew it saw him, somehow knew he was there in the ravine. The beast above just stood, waiting for its partner to come out and they would both tear Josh apart. Josh watched as the beast reached for something inside its hulking darkness. Whatever it was, it pulled out in a closed fist then slowly opening it, waving its hand over the hole. Josh watched as these little black dots fell over the entrance and down the cement hole. They looked like millions of black spiders in the moonlight, crawling feverishly into the tunnel. The splashing suddenly stopped and the most horrible scream echoed Towaco, just bellowing out into the darkness, sending horrible chills up Josh's neck. Suddenly the beast above threw a sharp black finger towards him and shouted: "GO! NOW!" The haunting voice was all he needed to hear. Josh turned and headed into the blackness of the gully, away from the two creatures behind him. He ran and ran, till he came to the sharp bend of the flowing stream—he turned, hiding behind the embankment, looking around a corner as the screams faded in the distance. No one was following him, no dark beast there to drag him into the pipe. Feeling somewhat relaxed, he felt a lavender fog touch his cheek. He saw the fog drifting in the ditch, just a slowly flowing incandescent, lavender glow. Josh lost all fear as he moved his hand through the smoky fog; it twirled around his fingers, losing himself for a moment and then moving into it.

He walked further into the woods, following the strange fog. He was not scared because the fog illuminated the dark woods into wonderful purples and blues, bringing it to life in a way totally alien to this world. Sometimes he would stop and just watch it curl, bend and float through the different organic things growing and living around him. It is a very chilly night, but the fog, somehow, keeps him warm and relaxed. Then, in the distance, he can see a white light glowing in the woods. He knew exactly where it was coming from—Herman's pond.

He moved slowly towards the glowing light off in the distance, periodically looking down at his feet, making sure not to trip on any debris, or step into the flowing, silver stream. He moved on, blinking from the brightness, but nonetheless smiling, not even knowing why. The ditch was getting narrower as he moved deeper into the woods. The ditch is now level with his head, he can see over its edge.

Josh suddenly thought of his mother. He knows she is going to miss him terribly, but if she only knew where he was going. He didn't fully understand, but he knew it was wonderful. He knew this is where people go when they die—this has got to be the doorway to heaven.

A sudden movement up front of him brought him back from his thoughts. The ditch comes to a T and splitting the flowing water into littler, streams disappearing into the night. This is where the fog stays, and right in front of him is Herman's pond. He heard music, some type of music very foreign to his ears, but ever so soothing. It is drifting over the banks just like the flowing fog. The fog was the music Josh realized. The bank here was even lower; he leaned on the cold embankment trying to see what is making strange scraping sounds over the edge of the embankment. He looks, through the broken view caused by the overgrowth, he sees her. His eyes went wide; they began to tear from a sudden blast of cool wind. He pushed some of the foliage out of his way, there, on the ice, was the most beautiful girl he had ever seen. She was ice-skating in the illumination of lights around her. The fog is being manifested through the ice of the pond. It was thick and foamy on top of the ice, you barely saw her skates touching as the purplish fog drifted over the bank of the stream like a slow moving waterfall, slowly drifting out into the woods. Yes Josh thought, the music was the fog, you could barely hear it, but when it touched you, you heard it fully in your mind. It was a haunting feeling, something so unnatural. Josh felt the separation, a paradox shift, the dividing of the two realities. He can actually see the two worlds divided. Looking out to the light of his world is dim, stale, like the sole light burning in a closet with just enough watts to see what you are rummaging for. This world, the one he stands in now is bright and somehow, alive. It seems to breath and pulse, absorbing the air. It's like a doorway dividing two places—a place so wonderful, so exhilarating, a place he suddenly realizes, he does not want to be—if it means he has to leave his family—if it means he has to die.

Josh lost focus for a moment, losing himself in the music that is swirling around his mind. Shaking it off, he hears a voice almost as soothing as the music.

"Hello, Josh, I have been waiting for you."

Josh tries to focus on where the voice came from. He was looking through the many symmetries of the landscape, trying to see the face of the voice.

"Here I am."

Josh had seen her in an instant. He could only see her eyes but that's all he needed to see to be overwhelmed by their beauty. The blue of her pupils stuck out in all the whiteness that surrounded them. The blue of her eyes were strange, yes, they were beautiful, but very strange.

"Just over here, come to me."

He nodded without even thinking of what she said. He looked to his left, down into one of the T's of the stream, and saw a blue staircase going over the bank. It wasn't there before he thought as he watched the fog coil around it, seeming to materialize from her thoughts. He moved towards it, touching it to see if it was real—the cold railing told him it was. He ran up the couple of steps quickly, not trusting the alien object, however it held firm. He turned to look at his surroundings, and it was just as he thought, totally amazing.

He truly stepped into another world. The first step was the hardest.

He felt a jolt of something alien through his chest as he stepped out onto the slippery ice, making him lose his balance and almost fall. The thick, lavender fog coiled his feet, the music of a distant world flows through him like an invisible wave wrapping around his body. It ran through him like an electrical charge, making him feel warm and comfortable in the chilly night.

That was only the beginning of the wonderful things happening. The pond is much bigger than Josh remembers, almost four times its normal size.

Spreading out in different spots of the pond and beyond were ice statues of many different and wonderful things. Ice trees from small to the size of full-grown oaks spread out in different spots—a forest of ice trees. Josh walked through this strange, frozen garden in awe at what he was seeing. Ice birds frozen in flight, deer and rabbits frozen in their natural behavior. Abstract water sculptures erupted upwards then frozen in their most daunting and volatile form, quite beautiful really. The trees were like clear crystals shimmering in the moonlight. Josh can even see birds and squirrels frozen high up on frozen limbs. The trees seem to never end, stretching upwards, high into the sky. Turning in circles, he slowly spins, looking up, mesmerized as to what he was seeing. He inhales deep, chilling air and lets out a cloud of frosted breath that turns to bubbles, the more he let go of deep air from his lungs the bigger the bubbles became. His chest suddenly heaved with laughter and he began spinning like a top with the fog twirling at his feet.

"Isn't it amazing Josh?"

Off in the distance, he sees the distorted form of a girl in white. Through the trees of ice, she was swirling and twirling about a hundred yards away. Feeling the smooth slippery bottom of this place, Josh moved slowly towards her, not to lose his footing. As he walked he touched an ice tree for balance and removed his hand quickly because it was far too cold to the touch.

Josh walked through the forest of ice until coming to a small opening where—she is dancing. She was ice-skating in an open part of the woods, paying no mind to Josh as she swirled back and forth through the low-lying fog. She did figure eights and jumps that were simply amazing to his eyes. Josh skated many times and has seen many skaters at the railroad pond off route 202 but her moves were totally alien to him, nonetheless flowing and beautiful. She did these moves for what seemed twenty minutes or so then finally glanced over at Josh with a smile. She was short, shorter than he, with her long brown hair flowing off her shoulders. She wears a white dress that reminds him of a nightgown but it is too beautiful for that. Strange, intricate lace ran everywhere over the gown making it glitter when the light of the moon hit it. It was very form fitting except where it began to flair at the waist, with the cut and design making it look like a snow flake. She slowly came towards him, drifting over the ice like the wind, so natural, so beautiful. Diamonds seemed to swim in the blue of her eyes. He can actually see the blue of her eyes moving, flowing. She stopped in front of him, curtsied, and bowed, not taking her eyes from his.

"Well hello, Joshua Weaver, It is so wonderful to finally meet you."

Josh didn't know what to say. He can't believe her beauty—he can't believe death was so beautiful.

"I am Renina—Renina the Ice Dancer" She said with a laugh and curtsied once more.

She looked at him smiling, twitching her nose slightly, reading his posture and finally taking his hand. "Come, skate with me."

Josh did without question. He is awestruck with her and what the deep woods behind his house have become—a magnificent, winter garden. He put his hand in hers; it was warm and soft like cotton. She laughed and gave him a little tug. He slid forward without moving his feet. His eyes went wide when he suddenly realized he was in ice-skates, they just materialized on his feet and it caught him off guard. He slid forward a little more using his one free arm for balance but stumbled anyway. However he is very experienced with skating and soon was in total control.

The moonlight casts beautiful shadows through the ice-limbs of the trees, magnifying and creating a kaleidoscope of images on the ice-floor where they are skating. They began slowly, just drifting in between the ice-trees and the ice-sculptures that were throughout this wonderful place—just drifting on the smooth surface that lay under foot. Josh stopped a couple of times to look at the sheer smoothness of the glass-like pond they were gliding on. The pond seemed a living organism. Ill-defined phantoms swirled and twisted underneath, but if looking straight down you can see clear through to the strange life in its depts. Glowing fish swam slowly underneath—zigzagging under a sheet of what seems like glass. He watched strange plant life swaying to a strange current just under the surface. It was alive; the organic mystery was alive and beautiful.

"Is this what heavens' like?" He said, finally looking deep into her eyes for the first time.

"A small fraction, this is just a tiny piece."

He looked away; off into the distance of the night, a bit farther out past the mysterious world he is a part of now, into the distance from where he came.

"When I die, will my family be ok?"

She turned to him, put a finger on his chin and looked straight into his eyes:

"Josh, no matter what happens, you and your family will be

OK."

"Come, Josh, lets skate some more."

He looked at her, nodded in agreement, she took his hand and off they went.

Josh forgot the bad thoughts he was having. He forgot about the Leukemia that is killing him, that surely will take him soon. They just skated and laughed and he was enjoying the euphoric feeling that's running through his body. The weakness that sometimes tormented him was far away, lying dormant somewhere deep down in his body. In the course of their run, they would break away and do little twists or tricks. Renina turned, going into a spin. Faster and faster she went like a top, making Josh light headed just watching her, then stopping on a dime, not even phased by the dizzying spin she just did. Now it is Josh's turn. Yes he could skate fairly well; however his expertise was speed, not grace. Playing hockey with the other boys of Towaco, there was no need for the dignity of style—but he was willing to try—so without hesitation, he began his embarrassment. Josh began with what he knows best. He took off as fast as he could. "Josh, you—" Renina started to say, but Josh was already off in full stride. He went zooming in between the many beautiful sculptures that stood spread out sporadically on the pond. Renina could only watch as he faded into the purple-bluish fog, shaking her head with a soft smile, she followed, keeping her distance so as not to disturb the acrobatic endeavor he was about to do. Faster and faster he went. The fog curled off him in distorted motion, the wind is making his eyes water; rubbing them he did not see the glass like oak tree in front of him. At the last second he turned, just catching his skate on one of its many roots protruding and disappearing into the ice of the pond. His blade dug deep into it, sending shards of ice fragments into the air. He flew for what seemed like minutes through the chilly air. Somehow in flight he managed to turn in mid air and came down hard on his butt. After the sudden pain, he opened his eyes; he was still sliding on the ice, looking up at Renina, who had her hands over her mouth. After the initial shock, she said: "Are you all right?" Then she began too laugh.

"I'm so sorry Josh, I can't help it."
Josh looked at her; he slowly came to a halt against a glowing, crystal boulder sticking out of the pond. "I'm ok." He said, leaning to one side rubbing his butt. Before he realized it, she was standing over him. She helped him up, and they sat on the beautiful transparent rock that he slid into. It was warm and that surprised him; it was already helping his bruised ego. They just looked at each other as she sat next to him, laughing while he adjusted the sore spot to a smooth surface of the boulder.

Even though Josh is embarrassed, he is still illuminated with joy. This reality he is in now is just too euphoric to describe. Josh realizes it is very dark in the outer perimeter of the woods, yet his present surroundings are illuminated, glowing and alive. It's like a division of two worlds and the one out there is temporarily shut down so this one may exist—needing all its energy to function. But then something strange happened. The glow of this world slightly dimmed and the outer forest became slightly active, like drawing the power from this frozen oasis. The most horrific howl came long from deep within the tree line. A hideous chill shot through Josh like an electric jolt, there was a definite distinction from the cool chill he was experiencing here and the jolt he just received. But he knew what it was. That bastard roaming the sewers and now, Josh just remembered, there might be two of them. A look of worry fell over his face. He turned to Renina who was staring into the deep night, beyond her oasis.

"Don't worry Josh, he can't hurt you here. Nor can the Witch."

Josh's eyebrows furrowed. "Witch?"

"The one trying to prevent me from doing my job—the one wanting the souls of God. But like I said, there is nothing for you to worry about."

Josh looked down. "I'm not scared! I got here didn't I?" A long pause then he finally said: "Will we be leaving soon?"

As she kept her focus where the horrifying wail came from, she said:

"No."

Josh jerked his head up, looking at her with amazement.

"There is unfinished business that you must take care of. This will be very hard for your family. Losing a loved one is not easy, believe me I know, I have been doing this a very long time, and the pain is unbearable. I come in the night without warning, take a loved one, and they never see them for the rest of their lives. I turn families upside down."

Now she was looking at the ground, very sad, tears were welling up in her eyes.

"But tonight there is a change. I still have to take people when its time, and most times it will be without warning, but not to-night." She stood, gently wiping the tears from her cheek, and leaned against an ice-tree. "I want you to go home and spend time with your family, especially your brother." She turned looking at him with deep sad eyes. "You can't tell him why, just be gentle, tell him sometimes people have to leave and go to better places, and tell him everything will be alright. It will, I promise you that. Will you do that for me Josh?" She moved back towards him on the rock. He looked lost, staring at nothing, feeling guilty even selfish for not taking care of that long ago, then looking up at her: "Yes, Thank you for giving me this chance"

She gave him a sad smile, touched his forehead, and said: "Goodbye Joshua Weaver, till we meet again." His world suddenly fell dark…

* * *

Joshua drifted into blackness. It was empty, void, yet a strange consciousness was there. A perplexing reality existed but for the time being it was incomprehensible to a young boys mind. In the womb of darkness, of peace, of null—say nothing, see nothing, hear nothing, and think nothing. This is the reality before consciousness, the place where true peace is understood. Consciousness is the worst thing that ever happened to man. It is the foundation for his ignorance and deceit to human kind. From the seeds of consciousness grows greed, anger, fear, hate, jealousy, despair, loneliness, love, kindness, happiness, joy—yes, one contradiction after another, but contradiction is also the fruit of consciousness.

But for now, he is nothing—his own being does not exist. So he thought—which was a very bad thing. However something began to happen—stirring in the shadow of his nonbeing—an echo from within began to tingle and vibrate through the nonexistence that he was. And that vibration grew steady with an organic shell molding to what was once a young boy named Joshua Weaver. The vibration began to form—an audible representation—it was thought that formed and converted into a comprehensible sound, now the understanding of words rolled through his newly forming mind.

"Am I dead?"

A foul odor began to fill the void of his empty reality.

It was the return of consciousness…

Josh woke with a gasping breath and a burning fever. He was hot and the sweat running from his forehead burned his eyes. He felt a cold hand touch his head, there was someone hovering over him in a blur. He blinked his eyes repeatedly; slowly an image began to focus. Muffled sounds were ringing in his ears. It was his mother over top of him with a look of fear in her eyes. "Josh! Are you alright?" She said, touching his head, cheek with nervous anticipation. She got off the edge of the bed, and started to pace the room.

She did that a lot these days.

"Oh, my God, Oh, my God." She said, mumbling over and over. Josh watched blurred auras trail off his mother as she strode franti-cally back and forth in the boys room.

"Where's Petey?" Josh slurred.

"He's in school." She said, not even realizing she said anything. She was lost in her thoughts, lost in her own commotion.

"What time is it?" He tried to sit up but couldn't get his shoul-ders off the soaking wet mattress. He was too weak to hold up his sweaty head.

She turned to him. "You stay in bed! You are not going any-where!" She sat down once more, feeling his head and cheek. "What time is it?" He said again, trying to see. "It's a little after noon." She said without even thinking. Suddenly the phone rang long and annoying from the hall downstairs. She turned white, with frantic overtones in her face, leaving in a hurry without saying a word, her shadows chasing her as she disappeared out his bedroom door.

He just stared at the ceiling. It was so distant, so far away. He felt the cold coming from the window, he felt it on the back of his neck and it made him feel even worse. He tilted his head slightly, this is all the strength he could muster to look out the window. It was a bright, sunny day. He could just see the top of the trees swaying back and forth from the invisible force of the wind blow-ing outside. His body ached like it never ached before, but sleep overcame him.

Josh felt a sting in his arm, opening his eyes wide. Dr. Gilda hovered over him with his thick, rubbery face, jiggling with his subtle moves, rubbing a cotton ball after the injection. The smell of alcohol and horrible, bad breath brought him fully awake. The doctor pulled back, and behind him was his mother with Petey clinging to her leg, staring up at the frightening, sloppy man called a doctor.

"He'll be alright." He said with a confused look.

"What's wrong with him?" His mother said. "It's not anything to do with—"

Rubbing his chin he said: "No, absolutely not." He interrupted, giving her a strange glance. "Must be the flu or something. Don't you worry there Nancy, I just gave him an arm full of penicillin— it'll fix what ever ails him."

Josh felt a pain where he received the needle. It took a minute after it was removed, but his arm began to grow heavy until it felt like a rock. However he didn't care. He just looked at Petey and can see he is still sick. He looks tired grabbing his mother tight, probably afraid he will be next in line for the needle.

"Just make sure he stays in bed, a good rest should fix him right up."

"Well, that's it for me, I must get back to the office. Nancy, would you mind walking me out? We need to talk." She just looked at him with not so much as a nod, pulled Petey from her leg and put him on his bed.

Josh knew their little chat was not going to be a pleasant one for his mother. Most likely, the quack wanted to discuss her overdue bills that are no doubt piling up. Irritated by the pain in his arm, he was just getting angry. But the burden on her will soon be over; the bills piling up will soon end.

Josh looked over and there was Petey looking at him with sad eyes. He is only four years old, yet he is so in tune with what is going on around him. After looking into his brothers' eyes, he remembered last night. It all came flooding back to him in one gigantic wave. He must talk too him, tell him how, sometimes, people must leave, and go to better places. Tell him he must take care of their mother, he must be the man of the house, but mostly, tell him that he loves him.

But somehow, just looking into his young, silent eyes, he knew all this already. He knew that after tonight he would never see his big brother again. Petey's eyes said a thousand words of pain. He had the same look when their father walked out on them a few years ago. Petey was so young, yet he had the same sad eyes he does now. He knew everything, but said nothing, Joshua's head started to spin, and before he realized it, the words "I love you Petey." Petey smiled a little, his face pale and tired, looking at his bed, then back at Josh, and then crawled in under the covers next too his big brother. Josh looked at him, then up at the ceiling and finally fell unconscious.

When Josh woke later, the outside was lit in white, luminescence from the low hanging moon above the tree line, like an incandescent flood light covering the world outside. He noticed the same, familiar purple glowing fog now drifting the darkness of his bedroom. The fog would swirl into angelic phantoms in the shadows—guardian angels, Josh thought, he felt no menace from them whatsoever, just a warm, soft feeling as the formed faces would melt back into the blending fog.

He sat up, wide-awake, like he's been awake for hours, the purple fog flooded into his mouth and nostrils in spurts with every breath he took. As mysterious as the fog was, he paid it no mind. He looked at the old windup clock on the dresser—it said midnight, Josh was asleep for hours and now all seems perfectly normal. While he slept, his reality ran through his sleeping mind. It wasn't a dream with pictures but just a knowing that flooded his unconscious—he knew it was time to fulfill his destiny.

Before he even realized it, he was dressed. He looked over at his sleeping brother in the shadows of his bed. He could barely see him, just the little lump of a child under the covers. The child made no sound, he knew it was useless to try and wake him, so Josh just bent over and kissed Petey's cold cheek and said: "Good bye, little brother."
This time Josh did not hide the fact that he was leaving. For the first time he actually heard his mother snoring over the constant humming sound coming from the TV—that black and white circle with an X in it signifying that broadcasting was over for the evening. He headed down the stairs and into the kitchen. There by the stove is his old friend Champ. His dog has been there his whole life, Josh cannot remember not knowing Champ, so alive for so many years and now, here he is, tongue touching the floor, eyes cloudy with death, Poor old Champ is dead. Josh kneeled, petting his old friend, with a tear in his eye, said goodbye.

Josh turned to the sound calling him from outside. It was the unforgettable sound of his old friend Champ barking from the corner of the house. He looked down at the dead dog, then out towards the back yard in confusion. Josh went out and just under his bedroom window, was the glowing silhouette of his dog. He looked much younger and more vibrant than he'd been him in years. The dog paid him no mind, he was just panting with tail wagging looking up at the second floor window waiting for something or, someone.

"I'm here boy, here I am." He doesn't hear him, doesn't see him. His dog, his friend is now in another world. Josh is startled to see the purple fog flowing out of his bedroom window like a slow moving waterfall, running down the side of the house, pooling around his ghost friend. He knew he was truly gone then, as the dog jumped around, his excited movements did not disturb the fog. Josh just smiled, he knew trying to have his old friend acknowledge his presents was futile, his dog was at the gate of another world and could not see him if he wanted to.

The blue alien auras coming from the woods caught Joshua's attention. It was so bright it almost hurt his eyes to look in that direction. He watched the mysterious fog that freely moved through the property now receding back to the woods, slowly fleeing over the garden and through the trees, back to its origin. Josh new his time was running out—he must go now.

But something suddenly cold crawled up his spine, from the old house across the yard, the screen door slammed in the darkness. Josh felt the evil in the air once more. However, now, Josh is afraid no more. He knows what was waiting there in the darkness. He can see both twins standing there in the shadow of the house. He moved slowly down the concrete stairs in their direction. Something twisting in the night caught his eye. Lily, with her white hair, walked out with a long knife in her hand, taunting and twisting the steal of the blade, catching the rays of the moon, giving him a good glimpse of it size. Josh knew the importance of fulfilling his quest tonight. The change in him that took place over the last few days has squashed all fear of the two evil ones. To him now, they were just two possessed little gnats that will not hinder him in any way.

Slow unrecognizable chanting began to fill his mind. Slowly it began to fill his head, like thick molasses filling the bucket of his mind. At his feet there were toys strewn everywhere by the porch. Josh knew what he wanted. He didn't need any light to find the handle sticking out of the old wooden chest. It was battered and warped but large and heavy. His Louisville slugger felt like an old friend in his hands. Pulling it out like the sword in the stone, this was meant for him and him alone. The steady chanting in his head subsided with confusion. He can see the girl's heads coming together with whispers filling his ears this time not in his mind. The confusion between the girls is evident. Josh moved towards them with the bat on his shoulder, the whispers were more frantic, and the shadows of their bodies moving with agitation. They twisted in the night, Josh kept coming, and the girls didn't know what was happening. A loud horrible scream came from the flood pipe down by the barns. It echoed hard and long, Josh knew time was running out. In the confusion, he saw the knife come over Lily's darkened head, and they both leaped for Josh. One swing and he heard Lily's jaw snap. He hit her and actually saw a flash from the strike. On the back swing he caught the other little girl in the temple, splitting her head open, it felt like hitting a melon as he watched the demon child fly against the wall of her house then lay there motionless—becoming part of the still, darkness of the night. Lily laid face down on the stone walkway with the knife still in hand, trying to get up but only managing to crawl a couple of feet, blurting something through her broken jaw, then fell face first into the stones. She was either out cold or dead, but Josh had no time to even care. He picked up the knife and started for the barns.

He ran hard, then slowing to the faint sound of a motor humming in the sky. He couldn't see it, but he knew what it was—the biplane is coming back—time was truly ticking away, he must hurry.

He ran passed the old, boarded up well and zigzagged through the five barns, stopping just over the flood pipe, panting hard and sweating profusely. He was glad for the pause to gather his thoughts and to capture some much needed wind while making sure the knife is firmly in hand. But the fierceness in his eyes would not budge from the entrance of hell he stood over.

A child's giggle caught his attention. He closed his eyes for a second and tears flowed down his cheek. He turned to the open field and saw the cause of the giggle and laughter. Petey and Champ were running and playing together through the open field. Petey was glowing in the night; so small, so content just laughing and giggling with Champ at his side, twirling excitedly. They were running through the field, heading to the woods, towards the glow just through the treeline. Josh stood in silence, pushing the tears away with his dirty hands, watching the two play-friends run down into the gully, where the purple fog met them. He watched the fog curl around their bodies then fading softly disappearing into it.

Josh heard the sound he was waiting to here. The splashing of feet in water, ran the pipe he stood over. Heavy breathing echoed through it sending chills up his spine. Louder and louder, closer and closer the sounds came filling the air. He looked towards the distant fog, looking for his brother, but he was too deep into it. That gave him a sigh of relief but nonetheless his blood was pumping. Dark clouds filled the sky; thunder rolled off the mountain, a foul odor floated on a strange wind and suddenly, in a burst of speed the beast flew out of the pipe. Running in full, lumpish stride going after something Josh thought was always him, but it wasn't—it was Petey he wanted—he wanted his soul for god knows what! He couldn't imagine this thing dragging his brother back into that hole; hearing the screams of his brother echoing the sewers of Towaco, no, it wasn't going to happen!

Josh began to follow the beast above the gully. He watched the black figure run somewhat fast, but with a strange limp, making it easy for him to keep up with the hideous humanoid. It splashed the cold water, soaking the shredded pants legs paying no mind to its surroundings, he was after the child, that was surely its goal. Josh kept a steady pace, not too close, but close enough to react if need be. He had no idea what kind of action he would take, he felt the cold, plastic handle of the knife in his hand, gripping it so tight that it started to throb.

Josh figured that maybe he would do nothing. Petey and his dog were lost in the purple fog, yet Josh could still hear his giggles from the distant, purple penumbra. The beast also hears the child's lollygagging up ahead and starts to move in hurried stride.

Josh looks over his shoulder to see if the other beast was anywhere around, but it wasn't. He knows now, he must act. He can't take the chance of anything happening to his brother's final flight.

Josh see's the gully narrowing up ahead; this is his chance to end this once and for all. He runs faster, timing the unearthly stride of the beast. When it was closest to the bank, he leapt into the air, wielding the knife over his head, screaming like a mad man, he came down on its back. The creature screamed as the first strike of the blade ran through the dirty flannel of its chest. He had a hard time pulling it out, but he managed. Before he could blink, again the knife came over the beasts shoulder, hitting it in the non-human flesh. Again and again, Joshua Weaver sank his blade into its chest as he road piggyback on a demon from hell. Its screams bounced the banks of the gully, frantically trying to get the boy off his back, but Josh withdrew and stabbed, withdrew and stabbed with chaotic frenzy! He watched the blood fly outward each time he withdrew the knife, feeling it rip the flesh as it sank deep with every new blow. Ten, twenty, thirty stabs—it doesn't matter, he just kept his steady repetition. His arm is getting weak from the constant thrust of his knife, the steadfast attack slowed, he suddenly felt his hair being yanked out by the roots. He managed one final thrust with the knife, with this he used all the force he possibly could, it wailed bloody murder long into the night. In the blink of an eye he was flying through the air, releasing the knife, leaving it wedged in the creatures bloody chest. Josh landed somewhere up stream from the beast. He came down head first into the cold, flowing water, swallowing what seemed buckets of dirty mud colored liquid. Hitting his head, on god knows what, he is seeing double. Frantically he tries to shake it off, the water is freezing and he began shivering. He is cold all over except where the blood is running down the side of his head, crawling onto a sandy bank, he is crying and gasping for air. The dirt dissolved with what is left of his saliva, making his mouth feel like he ate a box of chalk. He pulls himself up on the muddy, cold edge of the stream. Suddenly he hears splashing, knowing all too well who it was. Craven Dune was in a rage and surprisingly still alive. Josh began to panic, his lungs heavy with exhaustion, he tries to climb the embankment of the stream. But just as he is about to reach the top, he feels the all too familiar grip around his ankle. He tried to use anything for an anchor, all to no avail. The sudden burst of cold water engulfs him; he feels the tiny rocks from the stream scraping his stomach. He feels the hatred hovering like a dark cloud. Standing tall, right over the young boy was his worst nightmare. Blood from its wounds dripped on Josh's face. It looked like a road map running up his heaving chest. Josh pushed away the tears to see the creature. He slowly lifted his eyes up the torso of the beast that is going to kill him. His face is covered with wet matted hair, and above its head is a huge rock, dark and heavy. Josh turned on his back and tried to crawl backwards but couldn't. He was trapped at the edge of the rising cliff, with the darkened shadow of evil standing over him. The beast is bleeding profusely, trying to catch its breath, and probably waiting to gather as much strength as it could before delivering the final blow. Josh looked down at the creature's feet lost under the stream. If he was going to die, he didn't want to see it coming. A rainbow slick glowing from the moonlight was oozing from around the submerged legs—some type of oil was flowing down the rippling water. The smell of it was putrid; he couldn't take it any more, without looking up: "Just get it over with!" He screamed. CRACK! Ran through Josh like an icy wind. Still not looking up, not knowing what had just happened, another THUD! Echoed and the boulder that was meant for Josh's head, fell at his side. The creature fell into the stream; it lay there motionless, face down, its lifeless body dancing with the current of the flowing water. Josh looked up and his eyes went wide. A dark, shorter creature was standing over the other. It was similar to Craven, but something was different, yet, it was the same. It had the same spider-webbed hair, same grotesque features. In its hand was Josh's baseball bat, the same bat he used to break his cousins jaw was now used on Craven. The bat most likely would not have been enough, but the boulder Craven was holding over his head did the trick. It came down hard, ether killing him or just knocking him out cold.

Then in a fury, the smaller beast came towards Josh, he gasped for air, again trying to get up the side of the sandy cliff, but to no avail. The creature picked up the giant rock at its feet without any strain, like it was loaf of bread, turning to the unconscious Craven and slamming it onto his head once more. The sound was horrible as the blood shot up in the air, sprinkling like a fine mist across Josh's face. The head just bobbed in the wake of the disturbed water—the beast that was Craven Dune is now surely dead.

The beast that finished him off let out the most hideous and unnatural cries Josh had ever heard. It was long and chilling—he could barely stand the piercing sound. Then, in an instant, it stopped. The Town of Towaco was quiet once more except for an airplane flying overhead. The creature went over and sat on the bank where Craven lay dead. Josh could not stop staring at the beast; there's something familiar and it was haunting him. He knew it was time to get out of there but he couldn't move. It stared at the dead body for a long moment, trying to catch its breath, and then suddenly it took Craven from the water, and cradled him, caressing his wet, matted hair, softly weeping. Josh could only sit silent, staring at the two monstrosities in front of him. Suddenly in one breath, it stood, grabbing the ankle of Craven, and started dragging him towards the pipe way off into the distance. Josh couldn't hold back anymore, in a sudden spurt he said:

"Gretchen!"

The beast stopped without turning. Its hulking mass lurched in the moonlit night. He knew it was her, but what has she become? She still has the smaller, rounder, shape of what she once was, but now, like Craven, she is swallowed into darkness. Her cloths are ragged and torn, her hair matted and knotted. She turned towards him and in that instant, and through the shadows of her trans-formed face, he seen her eyes—humanistic, sad, and tired.

"Gretchen, what—"

"Like I said, when we are called, we go." The voice low and hideous, but the tone was definitely that of Gretchen Woodbury.

"But I—" He was interrupted once more.

"He is my son, Craven Dune Woodbury."

Josh was in shock he couldn't say a word.

She turned towards the drainpipe off in the distance, not looking at him.

"This is over, Josh, Craven is no more. She had me as long as she had my son. But he's free now, and so am I. The Witch will leave now."

"Go do what you must—go home."

She started off through the muddy water, dragging her once-upon-a-time son. She walked slowly to the entrance of an unseen hell. Josh could only watch as she disappeared into the darkness, the darkness of the drain pipe. He knew he would never see her again.

Josh snapped his head; he forgot all about his brother and started running towards the pond. He hears the soothing sound of the bi-plane once more. Running through the stream, he noticed that the beautiful, soothing fog that engulfed his world was now gone. The woods were returning to its original dark mystery that it always was at night. As he ran, the purple aura was retracting faster than he could run, the soft glow was dissipating and Josh was suddenly being swallowed into the shadows of night. Finally at the 'T' he saw through the very bushes that he first set eye on Renina, there she stood, hugging his brother with tears in her eyes. His brother was smiling, and seemed happy. He watched her kneel at Petey's side and point to the mysterious biplane over head. Petey just nodded with zealous anticipation of a child while Champ sat there wagging his tail wildly. Josh couldn't hear the conversation, even though he was somewhat close, he knows that the world they are in is closing, the glow of a beautiful place was fading away.

Josh said nothing as he watched Renina the Ice Dancer wave her hand back and forth over the ice where she stood. Glittering stars began too fall from her palm as she waved it back and forth. The stars began to illuminate and pulse with more and more falling from her hand. Soon they were engulfed in the perplexing aura of light. Josh could hear the plane getting closer. Suddenly from be-hind a low cloud, he sees it, way above the old abandoned airport of Towaco. He looked back, and now Renina and the rest were floating on a carpet of stars, drifting slowly up towards heaven.

The tears in Joshua Weavers eyes were flowing. The illuminat-ing cloud of stars is all he could see now, floating peacefully up, high into the sky. He watched the beautiful cloud touch the inter-cepting biplane, a soft glow erupted; the cloud of stars was gone, leaving just the biplane heading slowly towards the north. No tricks this time, no dazzling arrays of flight to tantalize Josh. It came just to pick up its cargo and leave.

Josh watched it for a moment, watched it fade off into the distant night. Everything now is what it was. The pond is what it was before Renina came, just an old, murky body of water in the middle of the dark, lonely woods.

Josh suddenly felt exhausted, it hit him like a large wave. He stops for a moment, feeling faint. He knows the night is not done with him, he must keep moving. Strange sounds caught his ears, a heavy whirling sound coming from the direction of the farm. He started running, running through the murky water, it splashed violently against him. Tripping a couple of times he finally made it up the embankment near the old barns. The barns stood tall, hauntingly in the night with its shadows from the bright moon painting the ground. The sound of the wind through the cracks and crevasses were like frightening moans, Josh covered his ears while he ran through the old structures. As he turned the corner the houses were in view, the wind was like a flowing river. The sky overhead was dark, the clouds whirling in all directions but the wind seemed concentrated, coming from one spot—it was coming from the well! He heard the cries of his cousins; they were hanging on the fence post in front of their house, screaming in terror. The first one to let go was Lilac, she screamed and tumbled towards the well, she was sucked in with a flash of lightning and the wind grew furious, worse than before. Her screams slowly faded as she fell into the black opening.

Lily hung to the fence post like a flag blowing in a storm. Feet stretched out with one shoe flying off into the stormy hell. She couldn't scream because her broken jaw was also flapping in the wind. But then something curdled Joshua's spine. Through her hair blowing across her face, she glared right at him. While her jaw was making silent uncontrolled motions—her eyes were hard and furious. Her jaw opened wide, wider than anything you could imagine. There, inside was nothing but blackness, a murky substance, foaming and gurgling then flowing out her mouth in a steady stream, off into the flow of the wind. The next instant, her jaw ripped from her face, and her eyes turned white. Finally letting one hand off the post, she shot Joshua the middle finger, and then off she went. No sound came from her, into the well she disappeared. The bright flash was almost blinding to Josh, but when he was able to look, she was gone. The wind died and the moon was once more beautiful in the sky—Towaco was quiet and peaceful. Josh looked up at his aunt's window, and he could see the fading black to white images of her TV flickering in her room. She slept through the whole thing as did everyone in Towaco. Josh walked in the now silent night of his home town. The back door was slightly ajar—this is how it used to be, people never locked their doors in this quiet town, it seems the serenity that made Towaco had returned. There is a soothing, deep chill in the air. It feels great against Joshua's feverish head.

"Joshuaaaaaa"

A voice in his head sent a chill down his spine. He turned towards the woods, looking for what he thought were his dead cousins. It can't be, Josh thought, it can't be! This voice however is different. It's not the dual, harmonic voices of the demonic little girls. This was a single, deeper, voice. He turned to the driveway and there, was his aunt, staring at him with demonic hatred.

"How dare you interfere you little son-of-a-bitch!"

"Everything was perfect, and now it is all gone. You ruined everything; those souls were mine and mine alone you little fuck!"

She spoke in his mind, her lips never moved. Her face distorted, it seemed to be bruising, bulging, and her teeth were spikes in her mouth. Without taking her eyes off Josh, the engine to her Sixty-Five GTO suddenly fired up, revving with anger. Josh looked into the windows of the car. He can see ghost-like shadows swirling and twirling like fog. He can make out some of the faces in the window. Bud the postman, Lily, Lilac, but not in their evil form, they looked like little girls again—scared little girls. His uncle was their and yes, even Walter Smith, distorted with fear. They all looked frightened, horror was in their eyes. He can see them all, trying to get out, trying to escape. They are trapped forever with the Witch as their master.

"You and I are not through, Bastard-Child, we are not through!"

Josh tried to speak; words were knotted hair balls in his mouth.

Her face suddenly softened, turning to normal, and this time she spoke, moving her lips as though nothing happened.

"Give my love to your mother, dear, tell her I'll see her soon."

"Maybe at your funeral."

She curled one side of her mouth into a crooked smile. The door to her car opened by itself, and she got in. As soon as she disappeared into the front seat, the car's tires spun in reverse, backing out the dirt driveway to the road. It sat there for a second, then off it went, heading north, laying rubber down Jacksonville road, driving off into the dark haze of early morning. Josh watched it disappear into a bend in the road.

Josh's mind was empty of thought. She should have killed him when she had the chance. She didn't, maybe that's not her thing. He knows it's over, for now anyway.

Josh walked through the kitchen, looking where his dog now lay lifeless, still in the dim light of the stove. Up the stairs he went to his mother's room. He knew she slept though the night, and surely it was not natural. How could anyone sleep through the chaos that erupted? There is no way. She lay there peaceful, beautiful, lost in a heavy sleep.

Josh headed to the bedroom he and his brother shared, he slowly pushed the door open and there, in the corner, lay the empty shell of his brother Peter Weaver, nestled in his bed, touched by the soft moonlight coming from the window. Josh touched his cold, breathless face and began to cry. He lies down next to him and cries like he never cried before. This is the closest they have ever been even though now, Petey is so far away. Then suddenly, the serenity of the house was interrupted, breaking the peace that was just restored after so long. Off in the distance was a sound that will save Joshua Weaver's life, but he doesn't move. Josh hears his mother getting up and rushing down the stairs.

He stays with his brother.

Off in the distance, a black rotary phone echoes the hallway....

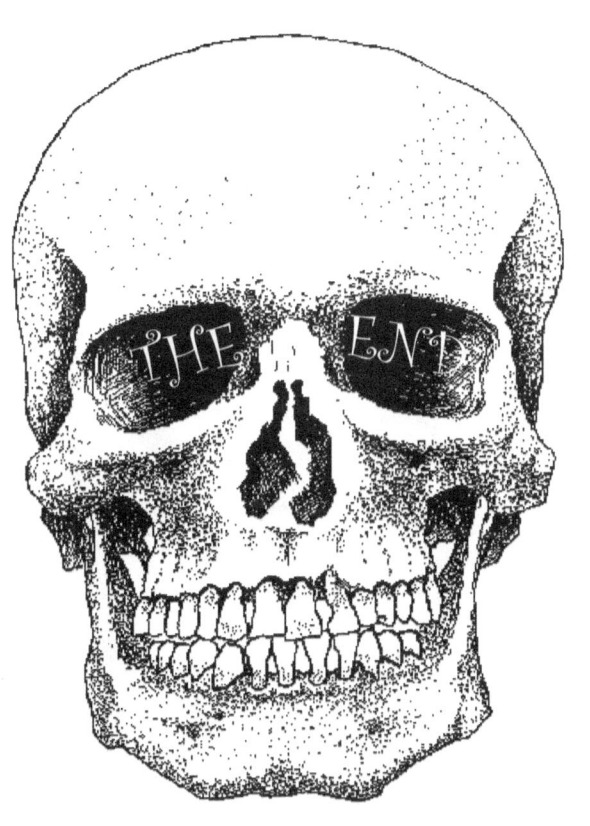

You can reach Errol in the following ways:

Snail Mail:

Errol Williams
C/O Waughaw Press
P.O. Box 1512
Rutherford, New Jersey 07070

Email:
pmm@errolwilliams.net

Web-Site:
www.errolwilliams.net